The CHOCOLATE Raccoon Rigmarole

Titles by JoAnna Carl

The Chocolate Cat Caper

The Chocolate Bear Burglary

The Chocolate Frog Frame-Up

The Chocolate Puppy Puzzle

The Chocolate Mouse Trap

The Chocolate Bridal Bash

The Chocolate Jewel Case

The Chocolate Snowman Murders

The Chocolate Cupid Killings

The Chocolate Pirate Plot

The Chocolate Castle Clue

The Chocolate Moose Motive

The Chocolate Book Bandit

The Chocolate Clown Corpse

The Chocolate Falcon Fraud

The Chocolate Bunny Brouhaha

The Chocolate Shark Shenanigans

The Chocolate Raccoon Rigmarole

Anthologies

Crime de Cocoa

Chocolate to Die For

The Chocolate Raccoon Rigmarole

A Chocoholic Mystery

JoAnna Carl

BERKLEY PRIME CRIME
NEW YORK

BERKLEY PRIME CRIME
Published by Berkley
An imprint of Penguin Random House LLC
penguinrandomhouse.com

Library of Congress Cataloging-in-Publication Data

Names: Carl, JoAnna, author.
Title: The chocolate raccoon rigmarole: a chocoholic mystery / JoAnna Carl.
Description: New York: Berkley Prime Crime, [2021] |
Series: A chocoholic mystery
Identifiers: LCCN 2021004449 (print) | LCCN 2021004450 (ebook) |
ISBN 9780440000273 (hardcover) | ISBN 9780440000280 (ebook)
Subjects: GSAFD: Mystery fiction.
Classification: LCC PS3569.A51977 C496 2021 (print) |
LCC PS3569.A51977 (ebook) | DDC 813/.54—dc23
LC record available at https://lccn.loc.gov/2021004449
LC ebook record available at https://lccn.loc.gov/2021004450

Printed in the United States of America
1st Printing

DEDICATED TO KIM KIMBRELL

Every writer needs a handy architect to answer questions,
and a brother can't say no.

The CHOCOLATE Raccoon Rigmarole

Chapter 1

I love coffee, but I don't usually drink it at the gas station with the guys. My husband, Joe Woodyard, also likes coffee. And at least five mornings a week he does stop for a cup at the coffee bar at the Warner Pier Rest-Stop out on the interstate.

And he does drink his coffee with "the guys," an informal group of old and new friends, most of them craftsmen, who have drifted together over the years.

Joe is six foot two, with dark hair, bright blue eyes, and the best shoulders in west Michigan. He has a dual career. Some days he goes to his boat shop and works on antique wooden boats, restoring them to their historic grandeur. On other days, he drives twenty-five miles to a midsized Midwestern city—Holland, Michigan—and there he practices law.

But in either situation—boat shop or law office—he almost always stops to have coffee, and maybe a doughnut, with the group known as the "coffee club." It's an informal group; Joe says one reason he likes it is that they don't have a constitution or bylaws.

I'm Lee McKinney Woodyard—early thirties, a shade under six feet tall, blond, and business manager for a company that makes luxury chocolates.

One morning in early summer I needed to hitch a ride into Holland to get my van out of the garage, so I rode along with Joe.

As we pulled into the Rest-Stop, Joe scanned the parking lot and took an informal count of the coffee drinkers who were already there.

"Tony and Digger are here," Joe said. Digger is a plumber, and Tony has a machine shop.

"Plus Mike." Joe laughed. "You can't miss that flashy GMC truck."

I laughed, too. "How'd Mike wind up with that red monster? Did he add the solid cover for the bed? It can't be standard equipment."

I grew up in rural Texas surrounded by pickup trucks, but most of them came with a folding bed cover made of vinyl—if they had any kind of cover at all. Mike's was one solid piece that opened like the hood of a car, and it was painted a brilliant red to match the truck's body. Add the giant tires and fancy steps, and Mike's truck yelled *Wow!*

"Mike swears he bought it secondhand and got a good deal," Joe said. "Of course, he uses that plain blue truck that belongs to the police department when he's on the job. The trucks that really make me laugh belong to the Vanderwerp cousins."

"I know," I said. "At first I didn't notice how alike they are, because they have those different magnetic signs." The Vanderwerp shoe store sign was red, and the doughnut delivery sign was blue.

"Yah. Funny coincidence they both bought white panel trucks."

R. L. Lake waved at us as he pulled out of the driveway. "Ooh," I said, "the doughnuts should be fresh if R. L.'s just leaving."

I knew all the coffee club guys, of course—or I thought I did. In a town of twenty-five hundred, there are few strangers. So while Joe went to the counter and bought a cup of coffee and a doughnut for each of us, I took a chair with the gang at the big table. Everyone nodded to me, and I spoke to each of them.

"Hi, Digger." Digger is a plumber, and he looks like one. Slightly grubby clothes, with dark hair and a thin face.

"Hi, Lee," he said. "How's everything?"

"Just fine."

I turned to the next guy. "Bill? How's business?" Bill Vanderwerp is an exception for the coffee club. He's a merchant, not a craftsman. Bill recently inherited a shoe store in the same block with TenHuis Chocolade, where I'm business manager.

"Doin' pretty good, Lee. You keepin' Joe on his toes?"

"Most of the time, Bill. We just saw your cousin pulling out."

Bill's cousin R. L. Lake, the other guy with a white van, had recently moved to Warner Pier and was looking for a house to buy. He was working for a doughnut shop in Dorinda, our county seat, making deliveries, and he usually managed to take his coffee break at the Warner Pier Rest-Stop while his cousin and his friends were there. I had met him only a few times, but I could spot him for a Vanderwerp: Warner Pier lore says they're all tall and blond, with friendly grins. Another tale about the Vanderwerps is that they supposedly expand as they age, so that twenty-year-old members of the family are skinny, but middle-aged Vanderwerps get well padded.

Bill and R. L. were almost the same age, but easy to tell apart. R. L. was the one with the bushy blond beard, and Bill was clean-shaven.

Bill smiled and nodded. "R. L.'s on a different schedule this week."

I nodded and turned to the next guy at the table. "Tony? How's it goin'?" Tony was chewing, so he simply nodded.

Tony Herrera and my husband have been pals since boyhood. Plus, they're stepbrothers, since Joe's mom married Tony's dad a few years back. Tony's a tall guy, too, but on the bulky side. His wife and I have been friends since high school.

Tony has a machine shop. I asked about it. "You still planning to bid on that big job?"

Tony gulped his doughnut down. "I'm still figuring, Lee." He gestured toward the final guy in that day's group. "Hey, you know Mike. He's joined us today."

"Gosh, yes!" I said. "How're you doing, Mike?"

Mike had once saved my life, and he was dating one of my close friends. Besides his gaudy red pickup, the main things that made Mike unforgettable were his looks and his size. Mike was six feet five inches tall and nearly that broad. His hair and beard, both cut short, were brilliantly red, and both curled. But his eyes didn't match each other; the left one wasn't shaped like the right one was. His nose leaned to one side, and scars marked the left side of his face.

No, I couldn't forget someone I owed so much or someone who looked like Mike. But that didn't mean I knew Mike well. Mike had a reserved side to his personality. He seemed to be hiding secrets I could never figure out.

I smiled, and Mike smiled back. Or maybe he grimaced. He

ducked his head and looked at a folded newspaper on the table in front of him. I saw that he was working a crossword puzzle.

Then a phone rang from Mike's direction. Mike growled and scowled. He stood up, walked a few steps away, turned his back on the table, and pulled out a cell phone.

"Bob?" Mike's voice always amazed me. He looked so tough I expected him to roar like a T. rex. But his voice was not loud. Still, in a small space like the coffee area, he was easy for everyone to hear.

"You got away before I could catch you. But I talked to Hupenheimer's, and they say they paid you two months ago."

Mike listened briefly, and this time I could hear excited noises coming from his phone. I couldn't make out the words, but the noises sounded just a little panicky.

Mike spoke again, and he sounded calm. Deadly calm. "Bob, I've killed a lot of guys for minimum wage. I'll be over to see you this afternoon, and I'm *not* bringing a lawyer."

Mike hung up, sat back down, and took a gulp from his coffee cup. His quiet voice had made his words truly ominous.

I shivered. Had I just heard what amounted to a threat?

The whole coffee club must have heard Mike's words, but nobody reacted very strongly. A couple of them cut their eyes back and forth, exchanging looks. Silence fell.

Then Tony cleared his throat. "Hey, Lee," he said. "T. J.'s talking about applying over at Ann Arbor next year."

I took a deep breath. "Joe's alma mater! He'll love hearing that! And getting a few miles away from home can be a good idea for any eighteen-year-old. But did T. J. ever find a summer job?"

"Yah." All natives of Warner Pier pronounce "yeah" as if

they're fresh off the boat from Amsterdam, even if their ancestors weren't Dutch.

Tony grinned. "His grandpa saved the day," he went on. "He hired T. J. for the night cleaning crew. Learning how to degrease a restaurant kitchen at two in the morning will make T. J. want to go to college for sure!"

That brought a few chuckles, and the conversation morphed into casual chatter about family and friends. Joe joined the group and sat beside me. He gave my shoulder a friendly squeeze and winked.

Nobody mentioned Mike or his dramatic statement about killing people for minimum wage. But I began formulating questions to ask Joe later. Questions about Mike.

And the first one I was going to ask was, Who was this Bob that Mike had threatened to kill?

Mike had moved to our small resort town—Warner Pier, Michigan—a little more than a year earlier. He came to work as a foreman on a construction project, but after that job ended, he had stayed. Mike didn't talk a lot about why he decided to do that, but we all knew he and one of my coworkers, Dolly Jolly, were a steady item.

Construction work in Warner Pier is not always available, so in addition to doing carpentry work, Mike had taken a part-time job as night patrolman for the Warner Pier Police Department. Currently, he didn't come to the coffee club very often because of his crazy hours.

Even though Mike worked nights and Dolly worked days, they seemed to be happy. I wanted the two of them to be happy. And I wanted them to stay in Warner Pier.

Dolly and I both work at the chocolate shop and factory

owned by my aunt, Nettie TenHuis Jones. At TenHuis Chocolade our motto is "Luxury Chocolates in the Dutch Tradition." I run the retail shop and the mail-order operation, and I order the supplies. Dolly Jolly is Aunt Nettie's chief assistant as a chocolatier.

Customers may look a little shocked when they enter our front door and see the two of us. I am five-eleven and a half, was born in north Texas, and think "you all" is one word. "Y'all." Dolly is more than six feet and a Michigan native. If strangers meet us standing shoulder to shoulder, they sometimes turn pale. I guess Dolly and I can make a big—yuk, yuk—impression.

Dolly and Mike make a striking couple as well. She has hair as red as Mike's, and her voice is as loud as his is quiet. But Dolly is a gentle, kind person, although she has a giant frame and a loud voice, and Mike seems to match her in personality.

So why was he threatening someone?

As soon as Joe and I were on the highway, I was ready for answers.

"Is Mike fitting into your coffee group?"

Joe laughed. "Sure," he said, "even though today he took on the role of our friendly neighborhood enforcer. I thought I'd told you about him."

"You mentioned that he had started coming to the coffee club when he could, but you've never said much about your opinion of him. I assume that you're kidding about his enforcement actions."

"Right. I can't imagine Mike hurting anyone, except maybe to protect somebody else. But I'm not so sure about his past activities in the field of killing people. He served around fifteen years in the army and flew helicopters in two combat zones."

"Ooh! I guess he's got the right to talk like a tough guy."

"Yah. I don't know who this Bob is—the one he was talking to today—but I'd advise him to get the money he owes Mike together. Fast."

"Does Mike have some connection with Warner Pier besides Dolly?"

"Yah. When he was a kid, Mike's parents had a nice cottage in Lakeside Addition."

"That semirural area? Lots of trees and two- or three-acre lots?"

"That's right. They were summer people while he was growing up. After Mike got out of the army, he started working in construction in Michigan and in Illinois. He inherited his parents' Warner Pier property last year, so he moved his construction activities here and became a local. When business got slow, he dredged up some training in law enforcement and snagged the job with the police department."

Joe's explanation had featured several local terms, since our end of the Lake Michigan shore has its own vocabulary. The people here, for example, are either locals, tourists, or summer people. Locals live here year-round; tourists stay a few days or a week or two; summer people stay all June, July, and August but live elsewhere between September and May.

Buildings have a special nomenclature, too. People live in cabins, which are rustic and may even lack basic amenities such as plumbing; in cottages, which are summer dwellings typically owned by the person who lives in them; or in houses, which are year-round homes.

Cabins, cottages, or houses can be any architectural style. For example, a home might have the steeply pitched roof of a mini Tudor manor, but if it's owned by summer people, it's still a cottage. Joe and I inherited the TenHuis family home, a typical Midwestern farmhouse on a three-acre plot, built in 1904. White, angular, two-storied—it's a house, not a cottage, because it has a furnace and some insulation, and we live there year-round.

After a moment, Joe went on talking. "As for Dolly, you know more than I do about what's going on with Mike and her."

I nodded. "She kind of giggles and blushes if his name comes up, but she doesn't provide many details." I considered Mike before I spoke again, carefully. "Mike's got a . . . distinctive look."

"I think that beat-up appearance is a souvenir of combat. Seems one of those choppers he flew for the army landed unexpectedly in unfriendly territory."

"Wounded? Tough luck."

Joe nodded. "From what he says, two of the guys in his unit had to pull him out, unconscious, and he spent quite a while in hospital and rehab. But Mike seems to be a pretty nice guy. I doubt we'll see an obit for somebody named Bob in the *Holland Sentinel* tomorrow."

We both laughed. The idea seemed ridiculous.

Joe's coffee club changes its makeup often. Sometimes I think all the guys have in common is a liking for coffee and another liking for doughnuts. And it's rare for all of them to show up for the club on the same day.

So far, no career women in our small town have asked to be included. Which may be a mistake on the women's part; the coffee club hears all the gossip first, and sometimes I get tired of getting it secondhand.

But on this particular day I was concentrating on my visit

to Holland. I forgot Mike Westerly as I considered taking time for a little shopping. In fact, I forgot Mike Westerly and his problems for about a week. And I didn't hear a word about anybody named Bob dying.

I stay pretty busy with chocolate. When they were young, my aunt Nettie and uncle Phil TenHuis spent a year in Holland—the country Holland—apprenticing in the chocolate business. They came back to their hometown as experts in truffles, bonbons, and beautiful molded chocolates—a perfect business for what we think is the best resort on the Great Lakes, Warner Pier.

I had worked at TenHuis Chocolade during my teenage summers, and after Uncle Phil died, I brought my accounting degree to the shop and joined Aunt Nettie. I hadn't planned to stay forever, but now I hope I can.

We've both acquired husbands who are nice guys. Aunt Nettie's is Warner Pier's police chief, Hogan Jones.

For marketing reasons, we do a lot of themes at the shop, and this summer's special chocolates centered around small wild animals of the area, using molds representing beavers, squirrels, rabbits, and raccoons.

My favorites are the chocolate squirrels. Somehow they taste nuttier.

I'd almost forgotten Mike making threats at the Rest-Stop until, late one evening a week or so later, the phone rang. Joe was working extra late at the boat shop, and I answered.

An excited voice boomed out. "Lee! It's Dolly! I need Joe!"

The fact that she was yelling didn't worry me; Dolly's always yelling.

"Hi, Dolly," I said. "Joe's not here. I can take a message."

"This is an emergency! Mike needs help, and he needs it right now!"

That made me a bit concerned. "Did you try to catch Joe at the boat shop?"

"No! I tried his cell! And he's not picking up."

"I'm sure he's on his way home. I can have him call you. What's the problem?"

"It's Mike! And this new sheriff! The idiot seems to think Mike is a burglar!"

Chapter 2

I tried to keep my voice quiet, the way Joe does. Every lawyer gets excited calls from clients. Usually Joe can calm people down by sounding calm himself.

"Where is Mike?" I asked.

"In our alley! Get Joe here quick!" And Dolly hung up.

"Dolly? Dolly?" I couldn't believe she had done that. I stared at the phone. "I need information! You can't just hang up!"

But she had. I stood there, trying to decide what to do. I was still staring at the phone when headlights bounced on the trees in our yard. Joe had come home. I could hand the problem—whatever it was—off to him.

Not for one moment did it occur to me that Mike could really be suspected of robbing somebody. After all, Mike was a friend. Also a cop, of sorts. Warner Pier paid Mike to *keep* us from being robbed.

When Joe came in the house, he wasn't happy about the message I gave him. He had already done a day's work in his Holland office, then skipped dinner to work in the boat shop for three hours more. He deserved food and an hour of sitting with his feet up in front of some mindless television show before he took a nice hot shower. A trip to help a—maybe—client was not likely to be on his preferred schedule.

But I fixed him a meat loaf sandwich, something easy to eat in the car, and volunteered to drive him back to town. In a small place like ours it doesn't take long to get wherever we're going.

Joe sighed as he climbed into the passenger side of my van and slammed the door. For a moment I thought he had merely wanted to drive. Like most men, Joe thinks that if the car is moving, he should be behind the wheel.

But a second sigh changed my mind. Then he spoke. "Thanks for the sandwich," he said. "I should have quit earlier. I'm tired. But I didn't see any excitement as I came through town."

"You wouldn't have passed our alley," I said. "So you couldn't have seen anything."

"And that's where Dolly said she was?"

"She said Mike has tangled with the sheriff, and something had happened in the alley behind the shop. Which, of course, is also the alley behind her apartment. That's all the definite information I got."

"Frankly, I can't think of any business worth robbing in your block. The only places that are open this early in the season are the shoe shop, the wine shop, and TenHuis Chocolade. But you don't handle much cash. And the other shops handle even less."

"True. Nearly all sales are by check or credit card. I hope this is a false alarm."

"I do, too. I consider both Dolly and Mike my friends. I don't want to find them in some big mess." Joe took a bite of meat loaf sandwich and used a paper napkin to wipe at a splotch of mayonnaise that had squirted onto his work shirt.

But when we got to the block where TenHuis Chocolade is located, there were a half-dozen vehicles with flashing lights in the alley.

"Bad sign," I said. "Some of those are definitely county cars. I guess the sheriff's here."

"I see the chief's car, too," Joe said. "And Mike's work truck is down there."

I parked my van on the side street, and we walked toward the alley. We'd taken only a few steps when someone called out.

"Lee! Joe!"

Both of us stopped and turned toward the sounds.

"It's T. J.!" I said. "What's he doing here?"

"Remember that he's on the late shift now," Joe said.

I groaned. "Oh yeah. Getting life experience."

Joe and I stood still and waited for T. J., or "Tony Junior." At seventeen, he now was taller than his dad, and he strongly resembled that member of Joe's coffee club.

Behind him was an older man, a bit shorter than T. J., wearing a black baseball cap. He was slightly built, making him look underfed to me. This was T. J.'s boss in his job cleaning kitchens. He had moved to Warner Pier only a few weeks earlier, but I knew him by sight.

The two of them weren't carrying cleaning materials, but the man had a small gadget in his hand. He put it in his pocket, and I saw it was a cell phone. "Interesting light patterns from all these cop cars," he said.

He turned away. "Come on, T. J."

"I gotta find out what's going on," T. J. said. "Joe, Lee—has there been a crime or something?"

Joe answered, "All we know is that somebody apparently needs a lawyer."

T. J. and his companion stopped a couple of yards from us, and Joe took a step toward the older man. "I'm Joe Woodyard," he said.

"Watt Wicker."

Joe offered his hand. "Mike Herrera speaks highly of you. How's your new assistant working out?"

T. J. ducked his head. "Aw, Joe. Watt's got better things to do than talk about me."

Watt and Joe both laughed. Then Joe turned back to T. J. "I'll leave a message on your phone," Joe said. "You get finished up and get home to bed."

"We're only getting started with Herrera's," T. J. said. "So we'll be on the job several more hours. I'm just curious. So many weird things have happened in the past couple of weeks."

"Really?" Joe made his own voice sound curious. "Are you talking about the invasion of the raccoons?"

This brought a snicker from Watt and a scoffing sound from T. J. "Aw, Joe! You know I mean the burglars. This gang has hit five or six places in the past two weeks!"

"The chief may not read it that way," Joe said. "Anyhow, if we find out anything interesting, I'll tell you."

"Yeah, T. J.," Watt said. "If Joe is here, I guess Mike will be okay."

Joe laughed. "You must have met my mother. She paid the bills for law school."

Watt nodded, but kept his deadpan expression. "Come on, T. J. We've still got two kitchens to do."

T. J. looked rebellious, and he was definitely muttering as he followed the older man.

Joe and I looked at each other and grinned. Yes, T. J. was getting life experience.

We walked toward the lights. A knot of lawmen and civilians had formed behind our shop. I could hear talking, loud talking. It was Dolly. Her voice was doing its usual booming, coming out of the darkness. "Mike was just coming to see me!" she yelled. "He drops by during his break!"

Then Mike spoke. "Dolly! I can handle this if you'll quit talkin'!"

But her voice continued. "This so-called law officer—"

"Dolly!" "Quiet, Dolly!" It took two deep voices to drown her out. There was a moment of quiet, and when someone spoke again, I realized it was my uncle—my aunt's husband—Police Chief Hogan Jones. Hogan's voice was quiet but firm.

"Dolly, you can have a turn in a few minutes," he said.

By now I could see the group more clearly, and I saw Hogan turn toward a man in a tan uniform. I recognized him as Ben Vinton, Warner County sheriff.

As Warner Pier police chief, Hogan is responsible for law enforcement in our small town, and he's hired by the town council.

The sheriff, Vinton, is an elected county official. He's responsible for rural areas and for small towns without their own law enforcement. He and Hogan frequently work together. Hogan wouldn't want Dolly to be disrespectful to the sheriff. He needed to get along with him.

Hogan cleared his throat. "Ben, I think this is all just a mix-up. Mike really is the night patrolman in Warner Pier. He makes two rounds a night, checking on the stores. I brought him around and introduced him to you last month."

"I remember. But why did we get a call tonight?"

Hogan's throat rumbled again, and he spoke. "We'll have to find that out. But first, maybe Paige here could put her pistol away, and we could ask Mike to stand up."

The sheriff looked around at the crowd. He seemed to shrink into his uniform. He had quite an audience of Warner Pier residents and law officers.

"It's okay, Paige," he said. "You've got a lot of backup here now. Put the gun away."

I turned to look at a new character. This one was a woman. She wore a tan uniform that coordinated with the sheriff's outfit.

"You're the boss," she said. Her voice trembled. "But this guy is big. And he's a stranger to me!"

Dolly's voice boomed. "Ha! Being big is no crime!"

Hogan didn't speak, but he looked toward Dolly and gave a glare that would have stopped a riot. Or incited one.

As Deputy Paige replaced her pistol in her holster, it seemed to me that both Joe and Hogan relaxed slightly. And I felt stupid. Until Paige was told to put her gun away, I hadn't even realized that a firearm was part of the scenario we were watching.

In fact, the light was so crazy that I hadn't seen either Dolly or Mike at first. Now I saw that Dolly was standing against the back door to TenHuis Chocolade, and that Mike had been spread-eagled on the asphalt pavement.

I knew both of them as law-abiding citizens. But if I'd been walking down a dark alley, I might not have wanted to run into either of them, given their sizes.

With Hogan sounding calm, and the sheriff backing him up, the situation sorted itself out. But Mike stood up slowly, looking as nonthreatening as a giant is able to. Hogan saw Joe, and used a nod of his head to draw him into the inner circle, introducing him as the city attorney, a job Joe holds as a volunteer. In a quiet voice, Hogan asked me to take Dolly up to her apartment and wait. Dolly didn't like that much, but I was able to nudge her into the TenHuis building and up the back stairs to her apartment. When she tried to talk, I shushed her until she began to make sense.

Apparently the whole brouhaha had started over a call reporting a break-in at the jewelry shop—actually the soon-to-be-opened jewelry shop—next door to our chocolate business. The deputy, Paige, answered the call. She had surprised Mike on his rounds and didn't recognize him. When she saw a huge man in the alley, she held him at gunpoint. Despite Dolly's loud objections.

Now two of the Warner Pier patrolmen and two of the sheriff's deputies were to be sent into the building next to ours to look around, and Hogan wanted me to keep Dolly calm.

When Dolly finished her tale, she threw herself into an easy chair, covered her face with her hands, and began to sob.

The sight of a weeping giantess scared me. I found a box of Kleenex in the bathroom and brought it to Dolly. She blew her nose loudly and rubbed mascara all around her eyes.

"Oh, Lee," she shouted. "I've made a fool of myself, and Mike's mad at me. But I was so scared!"

"Hey! Hey!" I said. "Let's start over. First, I smell codfish! I mean, coffee. I smell coffee!"

Like all my good friends, Dolly didn't turn a hair at my idiotic comment. I suffer from malapropism; this means I mix up words with other words that sound like them. The condition is named after a character in an eighteenth-century play, Mrs. Malaprop, who describes someone as being "as headstrong as an allegory on the banks of the Nile." I'm a direct descendant of Mrs. Malaprop.

So Dolly didn't reply directly. She said, "Yes, I always make a pot for Mike and me to share on his break. Would you like some?"

"Sounds great."

In nearly every crisis, I've noted, there are two kinds of people. Those who get hungry, and those who can't touch food. Dolly and I are both among the hungry ones. A cup of coffee and a Kahlua truffle ("a coffee-flavored interior enrobed in milk chocolate and embellished with a *K*") calmed the situation as we waited for news of what was happening to Mike.

"Since Mike works part-time," Dolly said, "he works a shift from nine p.m. until eleven or twelve. He takes a break. Then he works another three-hour shift." Dolly turned red. "And, well, he's gotten into the habit of dropping by here for coffee and a snack between the two shifts."

I assured Dolly that was a perfectly respectable schedule for a dating couple. She seemed reassured as she continued her story. Of course, I knew a lot of it already.

Warner Pier's regular police force consisted of five people—the chief, my uncle Hogan; three patrol officers; and a clerical worker. The police department office closed at five o'clock on weekdays. After that time, law enforcement was turned over to the Warner County Sheriff's Department. They had more staff and operated the county's 9-1-1 system.

During the past few weeks, Warner Pier had experienced a series of minor crimes. A half-dozen break-ins and burglaries had plagued our businesses. Merchants got nervous. They urged the city to provide round-the-clock law enforcement, something closer than the county seat.

Enter Mike Westerly, the former helicopter pilot who, as he had said, had "killed a lot of guys for minimum wage." Mike was eager to find a steady job in Warner Pier, and at some time in his life he had completed an approved training course for law officers. So Hogan hired him to drive through town a couple of times during the night, to check the entrances of businesses and to keep his eyes open for strange vehicles and suspicious circumstances. Mike also kept his eyes out for raccoons: darling animals who can be pests. Some victims had been blaming the break-ins on the nimble-fingered creatures. This was only sort of a joke, and the animal control department tried, not too successfully, to keep them from invading Warner Pier buildings.

At each of his stops, Mike would check all the doors and windows, making sure every entrance was locked as it should be and that any security systems were functioning.

Mike was sharp-eyed and smart, though minimally experienced in law enforcement. If he found anything strange, he called the 9-1-1 operator on duty, the police chief, or the sheriff. He wasn't supposed to investigate without calling for backup.

Mike usually ended his first patrol segment with a check of

the chocolate shop. I figured that he planned it that way so he could see Dolly.

I never mentioned those interludes. Mike and Dolly were both adults. I didn't ask any nosy questions, like whether or not they had discussed marriage. I considered that an extremely happy state, but they might not. For one thing, Mike had once revealed that he had gone through an unhappy marriage. He might not be ready to try again. It wasn't any of my business.

This particular evening, Dolly told me, proceeded as usual. Dolly heard Mike's truck pull up in the alley. This was the signal for turning on the coffeepot. But the next sound she heard wasn't so usual.

"I heard that deputy yelling," Dolly said. "She hollered, 'Hit the ground, mister.' And I heard Mike yell back, 'Hey, I'm from the Warner Pier cops.' They yelled back and forth. I ran to the bedroom window and opened it. And I could see what was going on by the outside light on the building across the alley."

Dolly quit talking and sighed deeply. "I guess that's when I lost it."

"Lost it?"

"It was awful, Lee. That terrible woman made Mike lie down on the filthy asphalt out there by the Dumpster. I yelled out the window, and I tried to tell her that Mike was not an intruder or a burglar or a bad guy of any sort! But she didn't even seem to hear me!"

I had to fight not to laugh. The idea of anyone who wasn't completely deaf not hearing Dolly's loud speaking voice, or her ultraloud yelling voice, was hysterically funny. But I gulped down my giggles and spoke.

"Did you call 9-1-1?"

"Of course! That must have been the first call the county got. Then I called you and Joe. But nothing seemed to stop her. And Mike—" Dolly's tears began to run harder. "Oh, Lee! Mike yelled at me. He said, 'Shut up, Dolly!'"

I handed Dolly another Kleenex and patted her back. And someone knocked on Dolly's back door.

Dolly jumped to her feet and shouted, "Maybe they've let Mike go!" I was nearly trampled as she headed for the stairway. I followed as closely as I could. Dolly yanked the back door open, and the two of us burst into the alley.

"Mike!"

But it wasn't Mike. It was another one of the sheriff's deputies. He fell back two or three steps as Dolly almost bowled him over. Faced with two towering women, he spoke almost shyly. "Ms. Jolly? Sheriff Vinton wants you to step over to the jewelry shop."

If they wanted Dolly, they obviously wanted me as well, or so I figured. The two of us followed the deputy to the next-door shop and went in by the alley entrance. We found ourselves in a storage area, a crudely furnished room lined from floor to ceiling with boxes. Two bare lightbulbs were the only illumination. Sheriff Vinton, Hogan, Joe, and Mike were all standing in a clump, surrounding the female deputy who had apparently started the whole commotion.

Hogan stepped toward us, while the others stayed back.

"Thanks for coming, Dolly," Hogan said. "We want to double-check a couple of things."

Dolly's voice boomed at its usual strength. "Glad to help! I'll do anything to get this mess sorted out!"

She had barely finished her sentence when a tremendous clamor broke out, and all the people in the room whirled toward the sound.

The noise was coming from the wall behind us, an area toward the front of the store. It was a heavy thumping sound. Bam! Bam! Bam!

I jumped all over. Dolly picked up an empty Coke bottle that was sitting on a table beside her and flourished it like a club. Joe whirled toward the jewelry shop cartons. Mike seemed to step back and put up his dukes, and Sheriff Vinton muttered an extremely impolite word. Only the deputy and Hogan looked calm; both of them gaped, but they didn't yell.

Joe was the first person to react usefully. "It's coming from back here!" He went to an inconspicuous door in the paneling, spotted the key sticking out of a small lock, turned it, and pulled the door open.

Then the banging became really loud. Paige pulled out a large flashlight, and Joe felt around for a light switch. "It's a storage closet!" Joe said. "And there's somebody in it!"

Joe, Mike, and Hogan crowded around the door. By pushing and shoving the other people, I was able to see what they were looking at.

A small man was standing inside. His hands were tied behind him. The loud noise had clearly been his feet, banging into the wooden door like a kettledrum.

Chapter 3

I hollered before anyone else.

"Alex! You were locked in!"

Joe and Hogan pulled him out of the closet. Hogan looked at Joe and mouthed the word "Who?" as he fumbled with the blindfold.

Joe answered. "Alex Gold."

I gathered that Joe and I were the only two people present who knew Alex. I turned to the sheriff. "Mr. Gold is one of our neighbors," I said. "Or at least he's a frequent visitor to our neighborhood. He's the uncle of Garnet Garrett. She and her husband, Dick, have a cottage across Lake Shore Drive from our place. Mr. Gold is a new business owner in Warner Pier. He owns this store!"

Alex Gold was a friendly, pleasant person, and Joe and I both enjoyed knowing him. He was a small-boned man in his sixties, no taller than five feet three. He'd be easy to manhandle.

How could anyone treat such a nice person that way?

As Joe and Hogan untied his hands and removed his blindfold, and someone got Alex a chair and a drink of water, I rapidly told the sheriff how he had recently leased the site of the jewelry store and was changing its stock to reflect the interests of Warner Pier.

"Mr. Gold is an expert on antique jewelry," I said. "Since Warner Pier is something of an art colony, he's remodeling the store to become a space for local artists and merchants to display and sell handmade and antique jewelry. He's been installing shelving and generally sprucing the place up."

While I was chattering to the sheriff, Dolly was quietly getting Alex Gold cold cloths. In other words, I talked about his need for care; Dolly actually did things to help him feel better.

Neither Dolly nor I offered to leave the scene. I wanted to know just what had happened, and I knew she did, too.

The explanation was simple, or at least that's what Alex told us after the EMTs had arrived and had assured the lawmen that he hadn't been seriously injured.

Alex said he had decided to stay at the store and catch up on some paperwork that evening. But first, he went down the street to Herrera's Restaurant for dinner. When he returned, he came in through the front door, walked into the storeroom, and found himself facing two men in ski masks.

"I didn't argue with them," Alex said. "I'm a middle-aged man who carries lots of insurance on his belongings. I work out occasionally, but I'm not going to put up a fight with two other guys. When the intruders motioned to indicate *Hands up*, I lifted my arms high!"

The two intruders locked Alex inside the little closet, using gestures to threaten to tie him up more firmly if he called for help or otherwise made noise.

Alex said he couldn't describe either intruder. "Both of

them were taller than I am." Alex shrugged. "But who isn't? All the men in our family are scrawny and short. Neither of them said anything. They communicated by gestures and shoves. Their clothes? Jeans and long-sleeved shirts, cheap stuff. No logos or slogans or anything. Both were fairly tall, but they were pretty broad, too. Heavyset. Actually I can't even swear they were men. Or even that there were just two of them. Once I thought they were motioning to someone else, but I'm not sure. But surely it was another man. I just don't expect that kind of unladylike behavior from women! I'm just glad they didn't decide to kick me down the basement stairs."

Alex gave a huge sigh. "What amazes me, though, is why they broke in right now."

The sheriff frowned. "Now? What was wrong with the present for a robbery?"

"The grand opening isn't for two weeks. We're still working with decor. We have no stock, nothing valuable here."

"So what did they take?"

"I didn't see them take anything! Honestly, I don't think they pocketed a thing." Alex pointed to the ring on his right hand. "They didn't even take this! An eighteenth-century gold signet ring. It's worth a couple of thousand! And I've still got it on my finger. They didn't bother to pull it off."

Paige took a deep breath. "Just like the other cases," she said.

Hogan glared at her. "We don't know for sure, Paige." Then he turned to Alex Gold. "Did you have any food in the shop?"

"Not really. I'm not a snack fan. But there may be something around."

Hogan and Joe helped him get up, and Alex went to a cabinet against one wall.

Alex began to mutter. "My niece has been eating her lunch here. She may have left something." He began to open and shut the doors of the cupboards. Then he turned around, holding an empty blue plastic sack emblazoned with large white type. He waved the container in the air.

"Aha!" he said. "Oreos!"

We all stared, but Paige was the one who spoke. "The Cookie Monsters," she said. "It was them."

The little group stood immobile for a moment. Then Hogan took a deep breath.

"Okay!" he said. "Everybody out! We're going to do a complete sweep. I want to catch those guys. Sheriff, can you call in the state forensics team?"

We all knew what he meant. Tonight's burglars sounded like the ones who had hit Warner Pier shops for weeks. One of the television newsmen had given them the nickname "Cookie Monsters."

Little was known about them except that they prowled around local businesses, taking nothing but snacks and junk food.

They took cookies from break rooms, chewing gum from secretaries' desks, gumdrops from penny machines, and suckers that were supposed to distract unruly children in business offices.

Sometimes a burglar alarm seemed to discourage them; on other occasions, it didn't. In Alex's case, his burglar alarm—standard equipment for a jewelry store, of course—had not yet been installed. But nothing of real value had been taken in any of the burglaries—so far. Junk food was apparently fair game.

The low value of the stolen items was giving the burglary ring a false aura of harmlessness, I realized. Intruders got into our shops and stores, but took nothing but a few doughnuts or a box of crackers.

It was a joke, even to most of the victims. "You've been burglarized? Was it the Cookie Monsters? Did they leave sticky handprints? Ha, ha, ha!"

But Alex Gold was going to feel different about them now.

Aunt Nettie and I would feel different, too. Equipment for creating snazzy chocolates is specialized and expensive. If the Cookie Monsters damaged ours, it would cost some real money to replace it, insurance or no. And if someone broke in and contaminated the chocolate—well, that would be a disaster I didn't want to picture.

We'd already discussed putting up cameras and alarms. Now I vowed to get that done ASAP.

In the meantime, things were exciting in the back room of the jewelry store. Alex's niece Garnet and her husband, Dick, rushed in. Garnet said one of the sheriff's deputies had called them about the break-in.

The Garretts, of course, were frightened. After Alex had assured them that he wasn't injured—"just scared silly"—the three agreed to go over to Hogan's office and wait for Alex to be interviewed there. Dolly and I were also nudged out the door. Then Joe and I stood by to make sure Hogan didn't want or need us further; it was pretty obvious Dolly and Mike didn't. They stood beside Joe and me, shooting uneasy glances at each other.

Hogan emerged from the jewelry store's back door, shaking his head. "This is sure a nutty crime wave," he said.

"A little too nutty," Joe said. "The attack on Alex is an assault case, not just a prank."

"I agree," Mike said. "I'm not assuming these break-ins are harmless. And don't tell me raccoons are scootin' around town, disguising themselves with their darlin' little masks just to get a snack!"

We all chuckled, but we also assured Mike that we were convinced that the culprits—whoever they were—were not kidding.

"And, Mike, I'm sure glad you seem to have beaten the rap tonight," I said. "What a confused mess!"

Mike made a face, causing his eyes to match even less than they did normally. "I guess I need to get out more," he said. "I'd have been okay if Deputy Paige What's-'er-name had recognized me. I thought my looks were pretty memorable—and I've met that dame before!"

"Well, you don't need to meet her in the future," Dolly said. "I've got a pot of coffee upstairs. Everybody, come on up."

Joe and I declined and started for the van, but Hogan waved us down. He moved close to us and spoke quietly. "I might call you," he said.

"We'll be up," Joe said. "What do you need?"

Hogan's voice was still quiet. "I've just got a couple of questions," he said.

We got in the van and left. When I looked at my watch, I was surprised to see that the time was only just after eleven. I would have sworn that we'd been roaming around downtown for hours.

Despite the presence of every law enforcement car in the

county, with accompanying noise and lights, surprisingly few people had gathered on Peach Street. I saw T. J. and Watt looking out the back door of Herrera's, but most of the other onlookers were people who lived in the apartments over downtown businesses.

We were nearly home when Joe's phone rang. "Can you get it?" he asked, pulling the gadget out of his jacket pocket and shoving it in my direction.

I grabbed for it, but I missed. By the time I had it in my hand, it had quit ringing. I looked at the screen. "No message," I said. "But it was Hogan."

"I'll call him as soon as we get home," Joe said. "But the next time Hogan needs help, I hope he wants to make a will."

"Aw, Joe. Wouldn't you rather study human nature than make dull old wills?"

Joe reached over and squeezed my hand. "I've rarely run into a will that was dull and old. And you're the one who would rather study human nature."

"This situation seems to have plenty of human nature to study."

Joe shook his head as he turned into our lane.

Chapter 4

In fewer than five minutes Joe was calling Hogan from our living room.

Hogan began with a question. "Where are you?"

"Home. Do you need us to be some other place?"

There was a long pause. "Not if I can see you there."

"Sure. What's up?"

"Maybe nothing." He hung up.

Joe and I looked at each other. "Huh," I said. "Maybe? Maybe I can make you another meat loaf sandwich. And open a beer."

"All I need to drink is coffee, but I'll take a sandwich as long as you have plenty of meat loaf."

"There's no point in making meat loaf unless you have enough for the next day."

I sliced meat loaf, and Joe turned on the outside lights for Hogan. And before I could get Joe's sandwich onto a plate, I heard a car coming up our drive.

"Hogan's here," I said. "Why did he want to meet us at home?"

"He could be trying to dodge Ben Vinton. I know he finds him something of a trial."

But when Joe opened the kitchen door for our visitor, we saw a second vehicle was pulling into the drive.

"Did Hogan say anything about bringing anyone?" I asked. Joe shook his head.

The two drivers were conferring outside their vehicles, and after a moment they walked toward the house.

Joe and I spoke together. "Mike!"

Then Joe called out, "Come on in! We've got lots of meat loaf sandwiches!"

Hogan answered, "I'll settle for a cup of coffee."

I was surprised, since I don't expect anybody at all to turn down a meat loaf sandwich. But I pulled out more coffee mugs, and we were gathered around the coffee table "in a whipstitch," as my Texas grandmother would say.

"Mike says he's got something else to tell me," Hogan said.

"May we sit in?" Joe asked. "Or should we scram?" We all looked at Mike expectantly.

Mike frowned—or I guess it was a frown. It's hard to tell with a rough-hewn face like Mike's. His brows slid together, his jaw clinched up, and he ground his teeth before he spoke.

"You two are welcome to sit in. I need to talk to Hogan without that idiot woman from the sheriff's office, and Hogan thought you wouldn't mind if we did it here."

Hogan gave Mike an intense stare. "You have the floor, Mike. Go for it."

Mike took a deep breath. "A sheriff oughta be a big guy with a white hat and a six-shooter. This man acts like a rabbit! If he had a white hat, it would need holes for his ears!"

This caused Hogan's jaw to quiver, and I knew that he was trying not to laugh. He spoke, but his voice wasn't quite steady.

"Well, Vinton's pretty inexperienced . . ."

"True! He just doesn't seem to understand what's going on. That's why I wouldn't say anything when he was there!"

"He did act funny, Mike. Tomorrow I'll try to get him to relax and tell me what's bothering him."

Mike ran a hand over his close-cropped hair. "Maybe you can get it out of him. But with him in such a state, I was afraid to talk, and there's a couple more things I should tell you."

Hogan took out a notebook. "That's why we're here, Mike. Why don't you start the whole statement over?"

"Start over?"

"Sure. Step by step. Start with when you reported for work."

Mike said he had signed in at the Warner Pier PD at eight p.m. The office was closed, of course, but he had a key. He looked over a few notes either Hogan or one of the patrolmen had left for him, then locked up and started on his rounds.

He turned to Joe and me. "Tonight, I headed south. Hogan and I figured out some routes that go by all the businesses, and I'm supposed to follow a different one every night. Also, I'm supposed to vary my times. Some nights I start the rounds a little earlier, sometimes later.

"Tonight I drove down to the south city limits and headed back toward the north. I made around twenty-five stops, kinda zigzagging through the town."

Joe nodded. "So you don't show up at the same place at a regular time."

"Right. Except—I do wind up close to Dolly's sometime.

She gives me dessert and coffee. I have dinner earlier, before I start the rest of the rigmarole."

He sat up straight and scowled again, daring us to comment on his personal life. "I don't stay at Dolly's place long!"

"That's fine," Hogan said. "You're supposed to take a break. As long as you don't get too predictable."

"Yeah! 'There goes ol' Mike. Must be suppertime.' Hope I'm not doin' that. Tonight, I hauled into the alley behind Dolly's, and the minute I got out of the truck, the excitement started."

Hogan held up his pen. "Did you see anything unusual before you opened the door?"

"Not before! The fun started *when*—when I opened it. I saw something then, or thought I did. But purty little Miss Paige started yellin' her head off."

Mike's face screwed up until he looked like an ogre who had smashed his big toe with his own club. Then he dropped his head between his hands. "That woman's crazy! How could she say she didn't recognize me when Vinton introduced me to every single person in his department! The two of us talked for about ten minutes."

"I wondered about that," Joe said. "In a department that small . . ."

Mike gave a vigorous nod. "Right! And let's face it! A mug as ugly as mine's not that easy to forget. Even in a dark alley. And what was that Paige doin' herself, sitting parked in a dark alley?"

Hogan spoke in his most soothing voice. "Mike, I sure understand how bad she acted . . ."

But Mike waved his words away. "That's not the problem, Hogan. I understand people can be scared or surprised or—

well, have some other trouble, but whatever caused her to act that way, it kept me from doin' my duty!"

"Your duty?"

"Yes, Hogan. I think I saw something! Just as I got out of the truck! But I didn't get to chase him, or her, or it, down, because of Paige!"

"Okay, Mike! Tell me, what did you see?"

"I think I saw somebody down at the end of the alley. Behind the shoe shop. Running!"

Someone in the alley? Wow! That was a real development! I opened my mouth to ask whom he had seen.

But Mike was shaking his head. "I didn't have a clear look. Paige—she began to raise a ruckus. And when she pointed her gun at me, I quit lookin' down the alley right quick!"

Hogan spoke very quietly. "There's something about being held at gunpoint that destroys your concentration, Mike. Think about it calmly. Picture it in your mind. Can you remember anything about what the person looked like?"

Mike gave a deep sigh. "I'm just not sure, Hogan. I could have imagined the guy. I think—think—I saw someone running. But it was dark. Maybe he was wearin' black."

The three of us looked at him silently. I knew Mike had been picked for his job partly because he had particularly good eyesight and steady nerves. I felt that anything Mike saw was likely to be a real thing.

But as he described it, the episode happened in our dark alley. Sure, there were lights here and there, usually over a back door, but could Mike really have seen anything? And if the cops searched, would it be possible to find any evidence there?

Hogan echoed my thought. "I doubt you imagined it," he said.

Mike raised his head. "To tell the truth, Hogan, I thought Paige acted so weird about the whole thing—well, I felt that she could be mixed up in the deal. Am I crazy?"

"Her behavior was definitely odd." Hogan pulled out his phone. "And it might be hard to find evidence in a place like that alley. But we'd better check. I'll call Jerry and tell him to hang around there until daylight. Then I'll get the state police to give that alley a once-over."

Hogan got up and went into the dining room, where he called Jerry Cherry, one of his longtime deputies, and held a quiet conversation.

Mike shifted his attention to me. "I guess you know you've got a critter under your shop's back porch."

"A critter?" I'm sure I sounded incredulous.

"Yup. I've seen it every night this week."

"What kind of a critter?"

"A raccoon, Lee. I think there's a dozen or so scattered around downtown. Urban raccoons. Mostly mamas. There's at least three living in that alley."

Joe and I began to laugh. "Oh my gosh!" I said. "We've had them out here on the lakeshore. But this neighborhood's semi-rural. I can't believe they've moved into downtown Warner Pier."

"Oh yes. You and Dolly be careful—and Mrs. Nettie, too. All of you need to be sure to make a loud noise as you go out the back of the shop. If you step on one of those suckers, you could lose a toe. They can be fierce. And they each have forty teeth—forty! Including four in the front that a vampire would be proud to show off!"

Hogan came back to find Joe and me laughing at the thought

of being attacked by a cute little vampire raccoon. Joe repeated Mike's report on the urban raccoons. Hogan smiled, but he also endorsed Mike's report.

"I knew there were some around," he said. "Animal control tries to trap them. I'll call about them again tomorrow."

"I may just hire somebody," I said.

Mike stood up and motioned toward the back door. "Listen, you guys, I guess that's all I had to say. Dolly's really worried about all this. I guess I'd better run by her place and try to calm her down."

Joe and Hogan walked out to Mike's truck with him and waved him off. But I was surprised when Hogan came back into the house with Joe. I was also a little annoyed. It was getting extremely late, and I had to go to work early. Still, I tried to seem welcoming. I even offered Hogan more coffee.

"Oh no," he answered. "I'm out of here, but I did want to ask Joe what he thought about the way Paige acted."

The two of them leaned against the kitchen counter, and both stared at the ceiling. Finally Joe spoke.

"Well, Hogan, I'm asking myself just what Paige accomplished by that little stunt."

"I've been thinking about the same question. You got an answer?"

"All I can see is that she kept Mike from chasing the—ghost? The phantom? The whatever it was that he saw running toward the shoe shop."

Hogan nodded solemnly. "Yep. And was that an accident? Or was it on purpose?"

Mysterious Food

The Chocoholic books use food for a background. In the world of the mystery novel, this classifies them as "culinary mysteries."

And one of the conventions of culinary mysteries is that they contain recipes.

When the series began, I immediately foresaw a snag. The featured food in the books is always "Luxury Chocolates in the Dutch Tradition." Their author, JoAnna Carl, practices fair-to-middlin' mom's home cooking in the American tradition. I couldn't create a luxury chocolate in anybody's tradition. What to do?

Aunt Nettie, my fictional chocolatier, is described as spending a year in Amsterdam developing this skill. She would have worked hours every day learning to do this. I did not have a year to spend. My deadline was nine months off!

But my editor was understanding. She suggested that we substitute "lore," or information about chocolate, for recipes. So I interviewed real chocolatiers and read lots of books about chocolate. It was fun.

Now and then I would throw in things I thought were interesting, such as Cary Grant originating the custom of fancy hotels putting a chocolate on your pillow each night. (I rather doubt Cary did this, but that's what the source said.)

After a few books, some recipes did creep into the Lore. But not one of them was for a "luxury chocolate." Yet if I met a reader at a convention, say, or at a book club meeting, she was extremely likely to tell me she really liked my grandmother's recipe for fudge. Very rarely did she mention the report that Montezuma drank chocolate spiced with hot peppers before he visited his harem. Readers seemed to enjoy the recipes, even though they were not for "luxury chocolates."

So for this book, all the Lore concerns recipes, not one of them for a "Luxury Chocolate in the Dutch Tradition." I don't have that particular skill, and I can't write about it.

But all of the recipes have been tested by a genuine American home-cookin' mom. Enjoy!

And the next time you pass one of those fancy chocolate shops, go in and buy something. When it comes to delicious, nothing compares to a genuine "luxury chocolate."

Chapter 5

Ghost? Phantom? They were getting too wild for me. Or was I simply tired?

"Okay, y'all," I said. "You think Paige is in with the burglars? That would be a serious matter."

"You're right," Hogan said. "I'll talk to Vinton tomorrow. Find out more about her. Her background and training." He grinned. "We'd better not send her up the river until we've figured out a little more. For now, I'll go home, let you two get some rest."

"Not yet!" I said. "I want to point out that Hogan said he wanted to ask us to do something, and he's leaving without doing it."

"Oh, it's just an idea I had," Hogan said. "I've been thinking about the coffee club you and the guys have, Joe. They're a gang who really gets around—including at all hours. You know—if people need a plumber, it may well be in the middle of the night. Could you ask them if they have seen anything suspicious?"

Joe and I both burst out laughing.

Hogan was not amused. "Why do you two think that's

funny? Lee, you and Nettie joke that the Warner Pier Rest-Stop coffee club knows all the news first."

Joe shook his head. "But we don't know anything about *crime*. We just know gossip like whose wife caught him at the Podunk Tavern having a tall one after he promised he was going on the wagon. Or who's getting his house painted because he and the wife are thinking about putting it on the market. Nothing serious."

Hogan lifted his eyebrows. "Really?"

"Hogan," I said, "you can't believe that anybody here in Warner Pier has anything to do with these silly break-ins. It's got to be out-of-towners."

Hogan looked at me. "If you heard a little item about whose husband fell off the wagon, who would you repeat it to? A friend here in town? Or a stranger?"

I ducked my head. "I hope I wouldn't repeat that to anybody. But you're right, of course. Maybe the coffee crowd would know something. I sure don't."

"Think about it."

I stared at Hogan. I shrugged. Then I laughed. "The only thing that's made me wonder lately—well, it's just silly. But maybe Joe found out what it was all about."

Hogan and Joe both frowned at me. "What was it?"

"Joe, do you remember the morning I went to coffee with you?"

"When we drove on into Holland? Yah, I remember. What about it?"

"It was Mike. He made that peculiar phone call, and he said he was coming to see somebody and he wasn't going to bring a lawyer."

Joe laughed. "I remember."

"Did you ever find out what was going on with that?"

"With what?" Hogan sounded a little impatient.

Joe repeated Mike's remark: "'I've killed a lot of guys for minimum wage. I'll be over to see you this afternoon, and I'm not bringing a lawyer.'"

Hogan laughed then. "So somebody owes Mike money. Did you ask him about it?"

"Nope. That seemed a little too nosy."

"He was talking to somebody named Bob," I said. "Joe, do you know who Bob is?"

"Nope." Joe shook his head. "Hogan, did you want me to ask him about it?"

"Probably not. I doubt it meant anything. But help me out! Just keep your ears open." Hogan looked at his watch and sighed. "If I leave now, I might get two or maybe three hours of sleep before morning arrives. But if either of you remembers any coffee club gossip—well, pass it along no matter what time it is."

We waved Hogan off, locked up the house, and went to bed. I was glad our bedroom was on the first floor; I was too tired to climb up to one of the second-floor rooms.

Yet I didn't sleep a nickel's worth that night. I had to get my worrying done.

After all, I was concerned about Alex Gold being tied up and shoved into a closet, about Mike maybe seeing somebody running down the alley, about Dolly's stress over his almost-arrest, and about the possibility of burglars hitting my own business, TenHuis Chocolade. Not to mention the chance that some of the silly gossip that bounced around Warner Pier might *mean* something—plus the reliable report that our store had a mama raccoon living under the back porch. Every time my eyes closed, they immediately popped open again.

I've always suffered from seasickness, and the way I tossed and turned that night gave me an advanced case of the queasies. By five a.m. I felt as if I'd been over Niagara Falls in a kayak. Twice.

By that time I'd been in bed a total of only three hours. That may well have been the reason I felt so rotten. I gave up and got up. Lying in bed any longer simply seemed useless.

I moved to the living room couch, pulled an afghan over myself—and the next time I stirred, it was nine a.m., Joe had left for his shop, and I was late for work. My day didn't brighten up until noon, when Joe called and asked me to go to lunch with him.

"I'm not sure I can," I whined. "I was so late this morning . . ."

"Hogan's invited us," Joe said. "He had a long talk with Ben Vinton this morning."

"Where should I meet you? I'll be there in five minutes."

I wasn't going to miss any available information about Deputy Paige—I still didn't know her last name—and the mystery of why she had been hanging around in our alley. As well as why she had thought Mike was a burglar when he had already been introduced to her as a lawman. Seemed as if he'd at least get the benefit of the doubt.

As Joe and I walked into the back room at Herrera's, I saw that Hogan was already there. I hoped he had uncovered something and was ready to Tell All.

I looked at him expectantly. "What's the tale on Paige?"

Hogan chuckled. "On Paige?"

"Yah," Joe said. "The more I think about it, the more peculiar her behavior seems. Does she have any explanation?"

"She and Ben Vinton are joining us. You can ask her yourself."

I yelped. "What?" Joe gave a low whistle. Then the waitress appeared.

Joe and I ordered quickly. But Hogan dawdled over the menu—a menu each of us had read so often that we had it memorized. He was obviously stalling, and I wanted to kick the guy, even if he was married to my favorite aunt. When the waitress finally left, Hogan spoke. "Here come Paige and her boss. I'll let them handle their own explanations."

So Joe and I sat quietly, biting our tongues, while Paige and Sheriff Vinton perused the menu the way Hogan had.

And I got my first real look at Paige. The night before, she had been nothing but a vague shape in the dark alley and under the harsh lights of the jewelry shop. Today I saw that she was a beautiful shape.

Paige was around five-six and curvy, with dark hair and dark eyes. I guessed her age at late twenties. Her hair was cut short, and it curled around her head. Her ears were small and well shaped. Her eyes were gorgeous—expressive and warm. Her hands, her figure, her face—every bit of her was feminine, dainty, and—well, beautiful.

Except for her wardrobe. Paige was wearing a standard sheriff's office uniform, khaki tan. The only thing striking about her outfit was her belt, which carried accessories such as a pistol, handcuffs, and a Taser. These items had probably cost more than the typical woman's jewelry was worth, but no one could call them attractive.

She also had a name tag. DEPUTY PAIGE TIMOTHY, it read. So now I knew her last name. I felt stiff and uncomfortable. I was still angry with her, and I didn't feel eager to let go of that resentment. She'd treated my friends Mike and Dolly poorly. The prospect of eating a friendly meal with the deputy wasn't pleasant.

After the waitress left, Paige looked at the sheriff. He nodded, and she spoke.

"I want to apologize," she said. "I acted foolishly last night, and I hope I'll be able to make amends."

I wanted to ask what the heck she'd been playing at, but I left the questions to Hogan. And he didn't ask any. All he did was wait expectantly.

Paige went on. "I'm new at law enforcement, as all of you will have guessed. My job as a deputy is an entry-level job. But I want to do it well." She smiled ruefully. "I want to be an asset to the force and to Sheriff Vinton. I guess I got too ambitious."

Hogan answered in his kindest voice. "There's nothing wrong with any of that, Paige, though it seems to have backfired on you. But how did you come to waylay Mike?"

"I have two friends who live on that block. Newcomers—they are newcomers to Warner Pier. Their apartment backs up to the alley. Their front door faces Dock Street, in the block behind Peach Street, and they have a garage that is reached through the alley. So they'd noticed Mike's pickup parking there frequently, and they didn't know what he was doing back there. I guess they did a bit of spying.

"I really feel dumb, but after they told me all this, I began to wonder what was going on myself. Especially after a couple of silent alarms went off downtown last week."

Paige hung her head and gave a shamefaced smile. "I pictured myself catching a criminal and making a major arrest. I realize now how unrealistic that was.

"But all this alerted me to the situation in the alley. So after I left my friends' apartment last night, and I ran into the suspicious pickup they had described—"

Paige rolled her beautiful eyes. "I made a complete fool of myself," she said. "Sheriff Vinton has said he will forgive me, and I hope that Patrolman Mike will, too."

She gave Hogan a melting look. A look with a lot of eyelash-batting in it. "I hope you will also forgive me, Chief Jones. And help me to become a conscientious and efficient police officer."

Hogan smiled. "Law enforcement certainly needs all the conscientious and efficient officers we can get," he said. "And I'll be glad to help you attain that goal in any way I can. But how about Officer Mike Westerly? Doesn't he deserve some help, too? And how about Alex Gold? He also needs help. After all, Alex could have been killed last night. We all got so caught up in the confusion with Mike that Mr. Gold was locked in that closet a lot longer than he needed to be."

"I'm willing to apologize to all of them," Paige said. "I hope they'll all forgive me."

Nobody pledged their forgiveness—I know I kept my mouth shut—but nobody formally refused it either. Hogan and Sheriff Vinton started chatting, and the tension at the table settled.

I did feel some sympathy for Paige. She sat silently, with her head down, and she had made what seemed to be a sincere effort to apologize.

So I did make a few efforts to talk to her. I learned that she had grown up in Kalamazoo, and she had majored in law enforcement at a junior college, working her way through school as a discount-store clerk. She was single and had a small apartment in our county seat, Dorinda.

We chatted, but I certainly didn't feel that we'd made any steps toward becoming friends.

After my first few questions, Joe carried the conversation, asking what had attracted her to law enforcement, which parts of her training she had found most interesting, and if she was particularly drawn to any specialty, such as juvenile work, sex crimes, or traffic control. Paige said she was undecided. She gave him the big eyelash treatment that Hogan had received, too.

I appreciated Joe's efforts to lead a conversation. I think we were all glad when the checks came. Hogan, the sheriff, and Paige stood up, shook hands all around, and said good-bye.

"We'll see you at three o'clock," Vinton said. And Hogan nodded. The three law officers left while Joe was still waiting for his change.

"Well," I said. "That was an interesting meeting. And I've got an important question."

"What is it?" Joe asked. "Not that I have any answers."

"Why wasn't Mike here?"

"Hogan told me that's what the meeting at three is about."

"Oh." I thought about it. "Maybe that's a good idea."

"I thought so. Mike's a great guy. But he can be hotheaded. If he wants to blow off steam, Hogan thought it would be best to give him the chance in a more private setting." Joe sighed deeply. "Of course, if Mike wants to keep this job, he'll have to learn to handle his temper. He managed to do it last night. At least he waited until he got to our house before he let loose."

I nodded, and Joe looked at the ceiling. "What did you think of the beautiful Miss Paige?" he asked.

"I'm withholding judgment," I said. "How about you?"

"No comment," Joe said.

"Really?" I said. "I thought you and Hogan were eating up her act."

"You thought it was an act?" Joe sounded surprised.

"I suppose she had every right to be nervous in this situation. So any uneasiness might have been perfectly sinister. I mean, sincere! Perfectly sincere." I looked at my watch. "But in any case, I'd better go."

"Busy afternoon?"

I stood up. "I have some important phone calls to make. I'm waiting to hear from the burglar alarm company, and I need to get a line on a raccoon trapper. And actually I think I need to stop at the drugstore and pick up some aspirin. Would you please watch my purse for a moment while I visit the ladies' room?"

Herrera's facility was usually clean and ordinarily uncrowded. I scooted to its door with my head down; the only surprise on the way was that I saw Paige in the main dining room talking to someone I didn't know. She didn't see me. I had thought she'd already left.

Two minutes later I was in the back stall in the ladies' room when I heard the restroom door open and someone come in. I guess I wasn't paying attention, because I didn't make the customary cough or clear my throat to inform new callers that there was already someone there.

I jumped when I heard a voice. "Yes, I'm still here," a woman said. "It went over like a charm."

Was that Paige's voice?

"They bought the whole story. I'm now known as ambitious, but not too bright." She laughed sarcastically.

It was definitely Paige. I pulled my feet up so that they wouldn't be visible if she looked under the door.

There was a long pause, and Paige spoke again, even more sarcastically than before. "Listen, Bob, I've done the stupid-broad act you wanted in front of some real idiots. Don't push me any further! I could reach the blowing point! I've got to run; Vinton's waiting for me."

She paused, then spoke again. "Of course I'm not going to drop it! Not when we're on the edge of a historic deal."

The door to the ladies' room closed with a whoosh, followed by a dull thud.

Chapter 6

What was all that about? I asked myself that while I washed my hands. Not that the answer wasn't pretty evident.

Paige's whole contrition act had been a fake. She was trying to convince the sheriff and Police Chief Hogan Jones that she had handled Mike poorly because she was overly ambitious. And that could be true.

But maybe there were other reasons. Who was Bob? It was a common name.

When I left the ladies' room, I was dying to tell Joe the whole story. But Joe was at the front door, pacing back and forth. He shoved my purse at me and said, "Gotta run." So I filed Paige's phone call under "later" and forgot it for the moment. But I vowed to tell Joe, and Hogan, about the episode the first time I could.

As soon as I got back to the office, I called Wildflower Hill. The person, not the place.

Sometime back in the hippie era, a group of nontraditional people moved to a plot of land east of Warner Pier. One of the women had inherited the wooded tract, and they planned to form a commune and live there. They were going to be raising tomatoes and strawberries, and they pledged to live the simple life.

But they discovered that life is just not that simple. The tomatoes and strawberries didn't grow well. The commune members began to realize they might be able to live their simple lives in the woods and fields, true, but they were going to need day jobs as well. Eventually most of them left. One of the few who stayed—Wildflower Hill—trained to become a taxidermist and opened a business.

Wildflower had been the original owner of the property, and its ownership remained with her. She continued to live there with, eventually, her granddaughter and great-grandson. I even hired Wildflower's granddaughter, Forsythia "Sissy" Smith, as a bookkeeper for a few months. We all remained friends, but Sissy left her job with TenHuis Chocolade to enroll in college. Now I rarely saw Wildflower, because she did most of her shopping in Dorinda, and I hung around Warner Pier.

By the time raccoons invaded Warner Pier, Wildflower lived alone at the former commune, now known as "The Moose Lodge." The name was nothing to do with the fraternal organization, but instead referred to a stuffed moose head that decorated Wildflower's living room.

Wildflower still ran her taxidermy shop, specializing in small animals and trophy fish. And through our friendship, I had learned that if anybody in Warner County had the lowdown on trapping small animals, it was Wildflower Hill. Not that she was a hunter herself, but she knew who was willing and able to trap animals.

Wildflower seemed happy to hear from me. After a few

minutes of chatting about Sissy and her son, we got around to the problem at hand.

"Hey, Wildflower," I said, "we've got a raccoon problem."

"I've got a nice one in my showroom," she said. "But I don't think it's for sale."

"I don't think the one I have is for sale either," I said. "But it's living under the back steps at TenHuis Chocolade, and I'd sure like it to live somewhere else."

She whistled. "An urban raccoon? I hear that they're incredibly hard to get rid of." Her voice became suspicious. "You don't want to go the poison route, do you?"

"No. I'm not saying that's never the solution, but I'd rather just encourage the raccoon to move away. I'm not crazy about putting out poison in or near a food-production facility."

"Hmm," Wildflower said.

"Is there anybody around Warner Pier who would be willing to relocate a raccoon?" I asked. "I know some companies advertise, but could you recommend any of them?"

"I think the person you need is in Warner Pier. Try Watt Wicker."

"Watt Wicker? I don't think I know him."

"You ought to know him; he works for your father-in-law. Hey, Lee, a client just drove in. I'll talk to you later."

She hung up, leaving me confused.

The raccoon catcher worked for my father-in-law? For a moment I couldn't even think who my father-in-law was.

My father-in-law would be Joe's father. But Joe's dad died when Joe was in kindergarten. Wait, my father-in-law would also be Joe's mother's husband. Joe's stepfather.

"Oh!" I said. "Mike Herrera!"

My relationship with Mike Herrera was further confused because Mike was also the father of Joe's best friend, Tony Herrera; he was the grandfather of T. J., Tony's son and kitchen cleaner for the three restaurants Mike owned; and Mike was also the mayor of Warner Pier. But I usually thought of him as just a friend.

"Ye gods!" I said. "Mike has a ton of employees!"

They included cooks, clerical workers, waiters and waitresses, dishwashers, bartenders, and even my close friend Lindy, his own daughter-in-law. Plus, Lindy and Tony's three children.

I couldn't recall any raccoon catchers among them. And the name Watt Wicker did not immediately ring a bell.

Until now. Suddenly I had a mental picture. Tall, slightly stooped, wearing a black baseball hat and sometimes carrying a bucket and a pail.

"Of course." I said it aloud. "He's the guy who deep cleans the kitchens for all three of Mike's restaurants. T. J.'s boss. T. J. introduced him to us last night."

Next step was a call to Lindy, one of the managers of Mike's trio of restaurants. Lindy said she would have Watt call me.

"Watt—and T. J. as well—work such crazy hours that I'm hesitant to call them in the daytime. You could call at three p.m. and get them out of bed. But Watt and T. J. have dinner at one or another of the restaurants every night. It's one of their benefits. Both are usually on the job by ten thirty or eleven."

"That's fine for me," I said. "We're always up late."

The evening grew long, especially because Joe did another one of his evening sessions of skipping dinner and working at the boat shop. The news from Paige—information I had eavesdropped on in the ladies' room—was almost forgotten because I never saw Joe long enough to talk to him.

I was still waiting to hear from Joe or from Watt when the phone rang at eleven p.m., and a gruff voice identified the speaker. "This is Watt Wicker. I hear you have a raccoon problem."

"An urban raccoon, Watt, if you can call Warner Pier 'urban.' Any ideas on how to get rid of one?"

"It's not easy. Do you want a live-trap job?"

"I'd prefer that. I'd also prefer that you have a place to move them that isn't our backyard. We already have raccoons at our house, but out there the wildlife and I sort of ignore each other."

"Ignoring usually works if you don't put in a garden or get careless with trash. But in town, it's different. Can I come by around noon tomorrow and look the situation over?"

I happily agreed to meet Watt at the rear entrance of Ten-Huis Chocolade. Joe didn't come home until I was asleep, so I didn't have an opportunity to tell him about Paige before I left for work. He was the one sleeping then.

By one o'clock the next day, I had struck a deal with Watt. He'd make the raccoon under the back steps disappear, and I would pay him a moderate amount of money.

"I appreciate you doing this," I said. "Raccoons are so cute that people always act pleased when they find one in their yard. But they're not pleased when they find out how destructive they can be."

"I've seen 'em tear up a whole set of outdoor furniture," Watt said. "They can rip the stuffin' out of cushions—just for fun, I guess. But I appreciate the work. Huntin' coons is more fun than cleaning grills. I just moved to Warner County, and a few local recommendations would help me build up that business."

"I could put out a flyer to all the stores in this block. Would that help?"

"I'll do it myself—after I catch your coon, Mrs. Woodyard. I can put a cute picture on the flyer, make people want the critters taken away and humanely released. It'll be more convincing if I can tell people I've already removed some from their neighborhood."

"Where do you take them?"

"Out near the Fox Creek Nature Preserve."

I nodded. Wildflower's property backed up to the Fox Creek Preserve.

Watt and I shook hands on it, and Watt used his phone to take some snapshots of food debris the raccoon had left in our alley after she dug garbage out of the Dumpster.

Then Watt climbed into the bed of his pickup and brought out the live trap—a sturdy wire cage with a small door. He placed it next to the stairs leading to our back door, a spot he said should be most enticing to the raccoon. He baited it with dog food he said he specially seasoned to appeal to raccoons.

I laughed. "That critter's taking my parking place."

"'Fraid so," Watt said. "But with any luck, it won't be for long. Just a few days."

"With the traffic in Warner Pier, it'll mean one more car in the municipal parking lot."

We both smiled, and I felt that I had successfully solved one of those problems they don't discuss in business school.

Only one surprise arose out of the whole deal. Mike Westerly also offered to do the job—for free.

I still hadn't had a chance to tell Joe about my arrangement with Watt. So when, at that morning's coffee club, Mike mentioned trapping the raccoon, Joe—my helpful husband—told him he was sure I'd take his offer.

I got the news at breakfast the next day. I was horrified. I couldn't have both Mike and Watt as raccoon catchers.

"Oh, Joe," I said. "I can't snub Watt! That's really nice of Mike, and I'd take him up on it in a minute, if I hadn't already talked to Watt."

"Of course you can't, Lee." Joe grinned. "You'll just have to cough up the money to pay Watt. Mike was simply offering to do us a favor. He won't be upset."

I growled. "Next time say you'll ask, okay?"

"Right. You stay out of boat repair, and I stay out of the chocolate business."

We shook on it. It was only then that I remembered to tell Joe about Paige's big reveal in the ladies' room. Joe immediately went to the phone to call and tell Hogan. This time Hogan was the person who couldn't be reached. Joe left a message, but Hogan was tied up with the state police detectives.

Changes are noticed quickly in small towns, so I wasn't surprised when Alex Gold called that afternoon.

"Lee! What's that wire contraption in the alley? I heard about it clear to Chicago!"

"The gadget is a raccoon trap, Alex. How'd you hear about it?"

"Bill Vanderwerp told me. Who'd you find to catch the critters?"

"We hired the guy who deep cleans Mike Herrera's kitchens. But how are you doing after your scary ordeal? It would take a long time for me to recover from being bound and gagged."

"Oh, I'm fine. I didn't need any special treatment; I'm just letting Garnet pamper me in my Chicago apartment for the week. Then I'll be back setting up the new store. But what's the raccoon situation?"

I chuckled. "Downtown Warner Pier seems to have a few."

"I have a family of them in the attic of the new shop."

"That's not good. Apparently this is a fertile year for the wild 'uns."

I told Alex about my deal with Watt Wicker and gave him Watt's phone number, warning him about Watt's odd working hours.

"I may give him a ring," Alex said. "I guess the kits are big enough to start scurrying around. The noise from the attic seems to be increasing. I don't know how they're getting in."

I pointed out that Watt hadn't yet produced any results from the trap behind TenHuis Chocolade. "It's only been a day," I said, "so that's not a criticism."

But I didn't get a report from Watt that day, and on the next day I grew impatient and called him.

"You've got a smart raccoon under your porch," he said. "She hasn't gone for the trap yet, but I haven't given up. I think I've found where she's raising her kits."

"Oh, gee! So she is a mama!"

"I'll try to snag the whole family. This time of the year the little ones are beginning to move around and follow their mama. I think one of them will go for the trap pretty soon."

Another day went by, and I could still hear the raccoon under the porch. Around eight o'clock that evening I called

Watt again. He didn't answer his cell phone, so I tried Herrera's Restaurant. Watt wasn't there either, but T. J. came to the phone.

"That's funny, Lee," he said. "I told him I was heading to Herrera's for dinner, and he said he wanted to check that trap first, and then he'd meet me here."

"That is odd," I said. "I called the cell number I have, but he didn't answer."

"I'll go over and check."

"Don't worry, T. J. I'll catch up with him tomorrow."

"It's time to go to work anyway. I'll find him."

As I hung up, Joe laughed. "You're nagging the poor guy to death, Lee."

"Maybe so, but if I can't park in the alley, I have to find a space in the municipal parking lot and walk to the shop. I'm tired of hiking half a mile to my office."

I settled down with a magazine for twenty minutes, but when the phone rang, I grabbed it.

"This is probably Watt," I said.

But when I punched the answer button, a woman's shrill voice hit my ear.

"Lee! Lee!"

"Lindy? What's wrong?"

"Oh, Lee! T. J. found Watt behind your shop. He's been hit in the head! He's bleeding! And he's unconscious!"

Chapter 7

At three thirty the next morning, five of us were keeping vigil in the emergency room waiting area at the hospital in Holland.

I felt so bad, I almost wished it had been me who had been found lying in the alley beside the live trap. After all, if I hadn't hired Watt to trap raccoons, he wouldn't have been in that dark alley.

But Lindy, Tony, Joe, and I had to keep up a brave front for T. J. He was only seventeen, and he had found his coworker stretched out, barely breathing, with a vicious wound to his head.

All of us had assured T. J. that he had acted exactly right. He had immediately used his cell phone to call 9-1-1, and Warner Pier's volunteer ambulance crew had been there within eight minutes. Lindy, T. J.'s mom, had waved at them vigorously when the ambulance pulled into the alley. T. J. had been kneeling beside Watt, applying pressure to the wound on the back of Watt's head with a dish towel. His own T-shirt, already soaked with blood, was lying beside Watt.

T. J. had called his mother, Lindy, who had been closing up

at Herrera's. She had run down the alley and waited for the ambulance with him.

Now T. J. spoke apologetically. "That T-shirt wasn't exactly clean."

His mother reassured him. "It was the best thing you had, until I brought a couple of dish towels over. Applying pressure was the important thing. You did a good job."

"He really looked weird," T. J. said. "The little raccoons were crawling around him."

"They had all stayed near the mother," Lindy said. "The five babies were all close to the cage, since the mother was inside it."

T. J. laughed self-consciously. "They scared me at first, because I couldn't figure out what they were."

He yawned then, and his eyes closed. I was grateful; he'd been so keyed up, this was the first time he showed any of the exhaustion he must have been feeling.

He slumped against his father, and I was glad to see that Tony—tough Tony—put an arm around his shoulder and just let him lean. When his mother took his hand, T. J. let her hold it, something he would never have allowed in normal circumstances.

I leaned against Joe, and he murmured in my ear, "T. J. will be okay."

I murmured back, "I know he will, but I'm really worried about Watt."

I closed my eyes for a moment, really no more than a blink, or so I thought. But when I opened them again, the whole scene had changed.

A giant face was a few inches from mine.

I jerked erect with a noise that was something between a yelp and a scream. It was sort of a "Yerp!"

But the monster had a soft voice. "Lee?" it said. "Joe?"

Joe apparently had been dozing, too, and he yanked away from me, jumping to his feet.

"Sorry!" The monster moved away, and when it was no longer so close up, it dissolved into the familiar and concerned face of Mike Westerly. "I didn't know you were both asleep."

"Mike!" Joe said. "I didn't know I was asleep either. What time is it?"

"Five a.m. Any news?"

Joe gave him a brief rundown on Watt's condition. "We're just waiting," he said. "What are you doing here, Mike?"

"I joined the search team," he said, "and we hit every inch of that alley. The sheriff came over, and his crews drove up and down all the streets to see who was out."

I spoke then. "Did y'all find anything? Anything that looked like a clue?"

"Very little. They found two teenagers driving a pickup that didn't belong to either of them. And when we aimed a flashlight behind a Dumpster, a bunch of shiny little eyes looked back at us."

"Nothing important?" Joe sounded tired.

Mike shrugged. "Nothing that looked or sounded like anything to me. Hogan sent me home, but I thought I'd check in here."

I settled into the couch again and tipped my head back. "Is Dolly okay?"

"I told her to keep out of it, and for once she agreed. She's staying inside with the door locked."

"Any security film from the buildings on the alley?" Joe sounded exhausted.

"Not so far as I know." Mike gave a big yawn. "Everybody's talked about putting in surveillance cameras, but nobody's done anything yet."

"We're supposed to get our system this week," I said.

Mike gestured at the coffee machine in the corner. "How's the coffee?"

"Black," Joe said. "Let's get some. Want a cup, Lee?"

I shook my head, and he and Mike headed toward the coffee. I must have dozed off again until I heard a polite voice. "Mrs. Woodyard?"

It was Paige. Deputy Paige Timothy from the Warner County Sheriff's Department. What was she doing there?

"I'm sorry to disturb you," she said. "Is there any news about the victim?"

"He's not dead," I said. "I'm afraid that's the best news we can expect tonight. When did you get here?"

"The state police took over the investigation, and the sheriff told me to leave. I thought I ought to tell you about the raccoons before I went home."

I sighed. The raccoons seemed to be the least important part of the situation at that moment.

Then Paige screamed.

It wasn't a loud scream, just a startled cry similar to the "Yerp!" I had given earlier. But it sure shocked me. My eyes popped open wide, my heart ran circles in my chest, and my breath came and went like a popcorn popper.

"What! What! Paige? Are you all right?"

She knelt beside me and whispered, "What is Mr. Westerly doing here?"

I stared at her and answered in a similar hiss. "The same

thing the rest of us are doing: keeping an eye on Watt Wicker. What's the matter?"

"Watt? Oh." She slid onto the couch. "I was just startled," she said. Now her voice barely trembled. "He's so big. He sort of loomed up. I wasn't expecting him here."

Looking up, I saw that Joe and Mike had rejoined the group. They gave Paige wondering looks before sitting down. Mike did look big in an indoor setting. I wondered if that was what had startled Paige.

"Mrs. Woodyard," Paige said solemnly, "I do have some bad news for you."

"It surely isn't any worse than the news we've already had."

"Somehow in the confusion of loading the ambulance and searching the alley—well, the raccoon escaped."

I thought about that a moment, then I laughed.

"Are you all right?" Paige asked. I think she was afraid I was weeping.

"I'm okay, Paige. That raccoon is the least of our problems at the moment. Thanks for telling me."

I had no idea why Paige had thought it was crucial that I know right away about the escaped mama raccoon. And I didn't care. I wanted to be home in my own bed. I would have said something else to her, but the doctor came in with a report. Watt seemed to be doing better. His head had quit bleeding, and he was conscious, but confused.

"We won't know anything more until later this morning. I suggest you all go home."

Joe and I left.

At ten that morning, we walked down the alley and looked over the taped-off scene of Watt's injury. All we knew about what happened was that somehow, Watt had been hit with a brick. One of the searchers had found it, still bloody.

"Is it possible," Joe said, "that this whole episode may simply have been an accident of some sort?"

"Sure!" I said scornfully. "We all know raccoons are expert climbers. Maybe ours simply scurried up to the roof carrying a brick and dropped it onto Watt's head."

"I doubt that," Joe said. "But she might have chipped out all the mortar from around a loose brick and asked her five kits to help her knock it down."

I rolled my eyes, and Joe laughed. "I guess I'd better not waste time speculating before Hogan shares his deductions. He has a lot more experience with this sort of thing than either of us."

This time we both smiled. "I'm just glad Watt is improving," Joe said.

"Yah. And that he knows who he is. Anyway, I'll see you at twelve at the Sidewalk Café. I'll call Hogan and see if he'd meet us there. Maybe he can introduce us to that brick."

The alley was a crime scene, so I walked down to the cross street, then turned right and went around to Peach Street, where the main entrance to TenHuis Chocolade was located. I was getting to the office late, and I had to catch up on work.

I hoped to see Hogan at lunch and that he'd have some rational explanation for the attack on Watt.

Maybe that would make me feel less guilty.

Chapter 8

The first thing I noticed when I saw Hogan walk into the Sidewalk Café at noon was how exhausted he looked. Since Joe and I had also struggled to get rest in the last few days, we were a grumpy group.

Lindy wasn't even in the restaurant; she'd called in sick. Her assistant, Dana, said that Tony and T. J. were also at home in bed.

Dana took Hogan, Joe, and me to the back room reserved for private meals. She seated our bleary-eyed trio at the table designed for groups of twelve and promised to send us coffee. As she left, she firmly closed the door that kept us out of the view of regular patrons.

While we waited for our coffee, I asked Hogan my first question. "Have you had an update on Watt this morning?"

"Same one you got, I think. He was better. Still dazed. Bad headache. Doesn't remember what happened. And beginning to worry about who's picking up the hospital bill."

"I'll have to check to be sure the shop's insurance will cover it."

Dana brought coffee and took our orders. Despite the time, we all ordered breakfast.

As Dana left, I asked Hogan another question. "Where did the intruders break in?"

Hogan picked up his cup and shook his head. "Wait a minute, Lee. Let's start at the beginning. First, *were* there intruders?"

"Hogan! *Somebody* hit Watt with a brick!"

"Are you sure? Nobody saw anybody. Unless you did."

"Heck, no. I wasn't there! But—well, I guess the previous break-ins in that alley made another one seem likely."

"No break-in has been reported. And while there were bricks in the alley, I can't prove that they were used as weapons. The whole incident could have been an accident."

Joe and I both shook our heads.

Hogan shrugged. "I don't think so either. However, Watt doesn't remember anything clearly yet. I might have to wait a day or two longer before we declare it an attack. He could have fallen and landed on a brick."

"All *I* know is that Watt told T. J. he was going to check the live trap," I said. "He apparently went behind our building where the trap was set up and then somehow got hit on the head. When T. J. found Watt, there was a bloody brick lying beside him, and the cops and ambulance crew found it there later. I'll keep calling it an attack."

At this point in the conversation, the door to the dining room opened, and Dana came in.

"Excuse me," she said, "but there's a man here asking for Chief Jones."

"Did he give a name?" Hogan asked.

She shook her head and moved closer to our table. When she spoke to Hogan, her voice had become a hoarse whisper. "He didn't give a name, but I know who he is. I've seen him on Grand Rapids TV. It's Phil McNeal!"

Hogan frowned, and I rolled my eyes. I had history with Phil McNeal. He and I had crossed paths several times in the past. Yet he could never remember my name or that we'd ever met before. In other words, I hated the guy.

Joe chuckled. "Hogan," he said, "you've hit the big time. If you make Phil McNeal's show, you are breaking news. At least in west Michigan."

Hogan was still frowning. "But do I want to be breaking news? Even in west Michigan?"

"I guess that's up to you," Joe said.

"There *was* something I wanted to tell the public," Hogan said. "Maybe this is as good an opportunity as any."

He stood up. "Dana, bring Mr. McNeal in, please. And tell the cook to hold my eggs until I talk to him."

Dana nodded with excitement. "I'll have him right in here."

As Joe and I grabbed our coffee cups and moved to the other end of the room, I said to Hogan, "You usually try to avoid talking to the press. You issue press releases. Why is Phil McNeal getting special treatment?"

"Sometimes law enforcement needs the press," Hogan replied. The door swung open to reveal Dana showing Phil McNeal and his cameraman in. Hogan greeted the Grand Rapids newsman with a friendly handshake. "Exactly the man I need to see," he said. "Dana, please bring coffee for Mr. McNeal and his cameraman."

McNeal looked wary. "You're probably aware, Chief Jones, that you have a reputation with the press for being tough to work with. So why am I getting the welcome mat?"

Hogan smiled. "For one thing, you got here before the sheriff."

The sheriff usually did the talking to the press.

McNeal beckoned to his cameraman to set up. He asked who Joe and I were, and Joe stuck out his right hand with all the airs of a small-town politician.

"I'm the city attorney," he said, leaving out the "part-time" adjective. "I'm just trying to keep up with what's going on around here. And this is my wife, Lee. The chief is her uncle as well as being our friend."

"We'll keep quiet," I said. "We certainly don't want to interrupt your interview."

In under five minutes, McNeal had Hogan facing the direction he wanted, and he had clipped a microphone onto his lapel. Then McNeal nodded to the cameraman and started.

"Chief Jones," he said, "we've been hearing rumors out of Warner Pier, rumors of a series of unusual break-ins at local businesses. Then last night, or so I understand, a workman was attacked, possibly by the burglars, and is now hospitalized." He leaned closer to Hogan. "Chief, just what is going on here?"

"Obviously, Phil, that's what we're trying to figure out. What makes these break-ins unusual is that although the burglars have gotten into about a half-dozen businesses, they never took anything of value. It was almost as if the perpetrators were showing off, trying to demonstrate that they could do as they liked. I think most citizens regarded the events as pranks. Of course, my department has taken these break-ins seriously all along, but we did not want to bring too much public attention to them."

"Why not, Chief?"

"Because the spotlight might encourage the perpetrators to commit more of these crimes. But now the situation has changed."

"In what way?"

"Recently, a local merchant surprised the burglars, and they locked him in a closet. And in a different incident, last night a man was seriously hurt. It's possible that his injuries came from a freak accident, but it appears more likely that they were caused by a deliberate attack, an attack that could easily have led to his death.

"We don't yet know whether there is a link between this incident and the burglaries, but in either case, we need to catch the perpetrators. So I'm asking Warner Pier's citizens and its visitors to help out."

"How?" McNeal leaned forward.

"Simply by calling us if they have seen anything unusual."

"What sorts of things are you interested in?"

"Anything out of the ordinary, Phil. A car in the wrong place. A light on in a building that should be empty. A pedestrian walking or loitering somewhere unexpected. We Warner Pier people are proud of our town. We think it's the most picturesque and friendly town on the Great Lakes. But we have a small police force. We need every citizen to help us find out what's going on!"

Hogan leaned toward McNeal and made his voice sound as if he were letting the newsman in on a top secret.

"Some local person may even be involved," he said.

Hogan assured McNeal that the identities of people who

called would not be revealed on the air. The interview ended with a phone number and with Phil McNeal grinning from ear to ear. He almost gushed with gratitude, thanking Hogan profusely for giving him the story. McNeal was still beaming as he left.

"Well, Hogan," I said, "you made his day."

Hogan gave a snort. "I didn't tell him I did the same interview with the Holland paper at ten o'clock, and I've got an interview with the Grand Rapids paper at two."

We laughed. Then Dana brought in our meals. We all grabbed our knives and forks.

"The problem with the Phil McNeal interview," Hogan said, "is that at this moment it's about all we can do—overtly—to find these jerks."

"What do you mean?" I asked.

"I mean the burglars are, frankly, much too sophisticated to merely be kids showing off. They've used elaborate techniques to open locks without leaving evidence. We know from the jewelry store incident that they've been careful to conceal their faces. Their vehicles have not been identified, though they have apparently been using a car or truck to get around town. They haven't bragged to their friends. Or if they have, the friends have kept their mouths shut. And they've resisted the temptation to steal valuables. They never take anything that has to be fenced, anything that could be used to track them down."

I stopped in the middle of salting my eggs. "Then why are they bothering to break in at all?"

"That's what bothers me, Lee." Hogan took a bite of his bacon. "Maybe I'm just a suspicious old coot, but what are they really up to?"

"They injured Watt," I said, "and the only logical reason was to keep him from seeing them."

"That's certainly a strong possibility. But we don't know enough about Watt Wicker to have a theory. It could be, for example, that Watt is an international crook and a rival gang is trying to kill him."

Joe and I stared at him. Then we both laughed.

"Watt?" I said. "That's ridiculous."

"Of course it is," Hogan said. "But what I'm saying is that Watt could have been the target of an attack for a lot of reasons. We don't know. But if people are willing to link the Cookie Monsters to this attack—well, let them. I'll investigate Watt without publicity."

"So all this stuff about people calling in is just so much eyewash?"

"No, we do need to know what's going on around here. If anybody has seen anything that might be linked to the break-ins, I want to know about it. I already asked Joe to mention the break-ins to the coffee club—those guys see and hear a lot."

Joe laughed. "As witnessed by the amount of gossip we spread."

Hogan grinned. "Exactly. But my first step will be investigating Watt Wicker. Where did he come from? Why is he here? I'm sorry this terrible thing happened. But what's really going on with him?"

Hogan stopped talking and took another bite. As soon as he swallowed, he motioned toward me with his fork. "So can you do a favor for me, Lee?"

"What is it?"

"Find out a little more about Watt Wicker."

"How would I do that?"

"How'd you find him? I mean, as a raccoon catcher."

"Wildflower Hill recommended him. I guess I could ask her if she knows anything about his background."

Hogan raised his eyebrows. "Go for it," he said.

1930s Chocolate

(The Chocolate Bridal Bash)

My grandmother was a fabulous cook and saw her family through the Great Depression by managing a bakery in Ardmore, Oklahoma. Here's one of her chocolate cake recipes.

Gran's Fudge Cake with Mocha Frosting

2½ cups sugar
2 sticks butter
5 eggs, separated
1 teaspoon vanilla
¼ cup cocoa
3 cups cake flour
1 teaspoon baking soda
½ teaspoon salt
1 cup buttermilk

Cream sugar and butter, then beat in egg yolks. Add vanilla. Add cocoa. Sift flour with baking soda and salt. Add to first mixture alternately with buttermilk. Beat egg whites until stiff, and fold in.

This recipe makes 4 layers or 1 large sheet cake. Bake layers 20–25 minutes at 375 degrees or sheet cake 35–45 minutes at 350 degrees.

MOCHA FROSTING

1 stick butter

1 egg yolk

4 tablespoons coffee

1 pound sifted powdered sugar

2 tablespoons cocoa

Soften butter, then mix all ingredients. Beat until smooth.

Chapter 9

I called Wildflower as soon as I was back at my desk.

"Hey, Wildflower, I need to know more about our champion raccoon catcher. Where'd you find him?"

"Watt? Oh, he came around with a big fish he wanted mounted. Then I helped him find a place to free the raccoons he'd caught. He did some trapping for a couple of the neighbors out here, and he did a good job. So I felt that I could recommend him. But what's happened to him? The gossip is that he was attacked."

"I really don't know the specifics," I said. "Hogan's trying to find out." I gave Wildflower a quick rundown on the action the night before and on Watt's current condition, ending with, "The doctors think Watt's going to be all right. But apparently he's not remembering much so far."

"Watt seems like a nice enough guy—at least, he's kind to wildlife and to old ladies. And he shows up when he says he will. I honestly don't know too much about him."

"Where's he from?"

"Someplace up north, maybe on the U.P."

I knew, of course, that the Upper Peninsula—the chunk of Michigan between Lake Michigan and Lake Superior—is a significant divide in Michigan.

Wildflower went on. "He's spent some time as a fishing guide, as well as in restaurant jobs. And I believe he was in the army a couple of years."

"Does Watt have relatives around here?"

"He's never mentioned any. Why all the questions?"

"The police are trying to figure out why somebody would hit him in the head with a brick."

Wildflower took a shaky breath. "I sure don't know. And I might not tell the police even if I did know! Just on principle."

I thought she was going to hang up, but I stopped her with a quick remark. "Wildflower! We're trying to *help* the guy!"

She gave a deep sigh. "I guess my hippie youth is to blame for my hesitation to tell the 'authorities' too much. But the person you should ask about Watt is Mike Herrera."

"Because Mike hired him to clean kitchens?"

"Yes. Watt was working for Mike by the time I met him. Mike would have checked out his references, especially before Watt started working with Mike's own seventeen-year-old grandson alone in the middle of the night."

"Good point. If Mike hired Watt to work in his restaurants in the middle of the night, with no direct supervision, I guess that's a pretty good reference right there."

But I was talking to the air. Wildflower had already hung up. I sighed. I made a note to take her some chocolates to thank her for her reluctant help.

When I first met Wildflower, she refused to eat refined sugar. But after a few gifts from TenHuis Chocolade, she'd become a fan of raspberry truffles ("dark chocolate center enrobed with raspberry-flavored white chocolate and embellished with a pink dot").

I already knew I'd have trouble following Wildflower's advice about speaking to Mike Herrera. He was out of town. He and Mercy, Joe's mom and Mike's wife, were at a convention in Seattle, representing Mercy's insurance agency. While I was sure both of them were packing cell phones, they still would be tied up with old friends and other convention activities.

My mind moved next to Lindy, Mike's right hand when it came to all three of the Herrera restaurants. She'd be in charge while he was out of town. She might well know a lot more about the hiring of Watt Wicker than Mike did himself.

Of course, just an hour ago, she had apparently been asleep, recovering from a night in a hospital waiting room. I hesitated, then decided I'd better call her anyway. To my surprise, she answered the phone.

"Lindy," I said, "if you're still in bed, I'm going to deny it's me."

"Heck, Lee, you can't hide that Texas accent. Besides, I'm up and at the hospital. Were you calling to check on Watt's condition?"

"Yes, among other things. How is he?"

"Much better. He spoke to me, and he knew who I was. But he's still groggy. The doctors want to keep him a couple of more days. Hogan called to check on him, too."

"Oh? Hogan gave me a few questions he wanted answered. I'm surprised he didn't ask them himself."

"We didn't talk long. He got another call and had to hang up. He just wanted to be sure that Watt wasn't going to be tossed out of the hospital immediately. But what does Hogan want to know about Watt?"

I explained to Lindy that we'd been so quick to assume that the Warner Pier burglars were guilty of the attack on Watt that Joe and I—and to some extent Hogan—had ignored the possibility that the attack on Watt had nothing to do with the earlier prowlers. Now we were trying to make up for our neglect.

My explanation seemed to leave Lindy more confused than ever. There was a long silence before she spoke.

"Huh?"

I started to speak again, but Lindy cut me off. "Lee, just cut the explanation and ask your questions." Then we both laughed.

First, I wanted to know how Watt got his job as night kitchen cleaner for Herrera's restaurants. Lindy told me that he had worked for her father-in-law ten years earlier. He came back to Warner Pier looking for a job.

"Actually," Lindy said, "he was looking for a job as a head cook. But Mike didn't have an opening. He told Watt that all he had right then was this cleaning job, and Watt took it."

"You mean, Watt had been a head cook, but he took a job as a cleaner? Working in the middle of the night?"

"Right."

"But why would he do that? And at the beginning of the tourist season on the Great Lakes? That's when people are fighting to hire experienced help. Seems as if there should be plenty of jobs around. With somebody else, if not with Mike."

"I don't know why, Lee."

"Hmm. Where had he been working?"

"I honestly don't know. The boss told me to hire him, and

I obeyed. I kinda think—I seem to remember that he mentioned working as a fishing guide. Maybe on the Upper Peninsula?"

"And he wanted a job as a cook?"

"He'd worked here as a cook several years earlier. I guess he'd decided he'd had enough fresh air for a while."

I chuckled. "So he turned back to grease?"

"Now, Lee—"

"Don't kid me, Lindy. I was a waitress nearly five years. I understand grease."

We both laughed. Then I spoke again. "Where does Watt live? And with whom?"

"I can't look his address up until I get back to the office. And he has never mentioned living with anybody. Listen, Lee, Mike usually calls me to check on the restaurants every evening. I'll get him to call you."

"Ask him to call Hogan."

We hung up. This didn't seem to be a promising line of questioning to me. Restaurant help has been known to drift from job to job. For all we knew, Watt's life might have been a series of temporary jobs and short-term relationships.

While I considered this, I started craving a piece of chocolate. I headed back to the workroom, picturing a milk chocolate raccoon, complete with sharply pointed white chocolate teeth and a dark chocolate mask. "Like a vampire," Mike had said. Maybe Aunt Nettie should have added a cape to her design.

Every TenHuis Chocolade employee was allowed two pieces of chocolate every working day. I never skipped either of mine.

With my raccoon in hand, I took a chair by Aunt Nettie's desk. "Sorry I've been behind on work," I said. "As soon as I get back from the bank, I'll start on the e-mail orders."

Aunt Nettie smiled. "Hogan said he asked you to make some phone calls for him. I know that slows you down, but he does need the help."

"So far I haven't learned anything very exciting."

"What is he looking for?"

"Some background information on Watt Wicker. I talked to Lindy and to Wildflower, but neither of them knows much about him. And Hogan and Lindy both say Watt is still pretty much out of it from his concussion."

I briefly described the few calls I'd made to find out more about Watt. "I'm sure Hogan has checked law enforcement records for a file on him."

Aunt Nettie nodded. "Maybe private employers can be casual about it, but the rules around background checks for city workers are pretty strict."

City workers? Was Aunt Nettie implying that we check out someone else?

My eyebrows knitted together. "Are you talking about anybody in particular?"

"Maybe Mike Westerly. We all liked him immediately. Everybody has taken him in."

"Oh." I thought about it. "Is that odd for Warner Pier?"

"Not so much these days. When I was a kid—well, you practically needed to provide your whole genealogy to get any kind of a job here. Even a job in the tourist trade. But us locals can still be pretty suspicious."

"People seemed to take me in without too many questions. Of course, I had family connections. And my aunt is the most popular person in town."

"And you began dating the most popular bachelor in west Michigan."

I smiled. "I still can't say 'yah' correctly, but marrying Joe makes up for a lot. I'd better get back to work."

When I stood up, my assistant, Bunny, waved from her office door.

"The deposit's ready," she said.

I waved back. "I'm on my way."

Aunt Nettie smiled her sweetest smile. "Take as long as you want. You'll be the one staying late."

My aunt is patient with me, but only to a point.

I grabbed the cash bag from Bunny, hid it in my tote, and headed for the bank, a block away. The short walk gave me a breath of air and a quick look at Warner Pier. I waved at my fellow merchants and stopped to chat with a few of them as I walked along.

Our downtown is small, only four blocks long and three blocks wide, but it's picturesque. A city ordinance requires that all new construction in the business district be red brick with white trim, to match the other commercial buildings. Everything a tourist could need is there—a drugstore with an old-fashioned soda fountain, a bookstore, two coffee shops, a half-dozen restaurants, a swimsuit shop, two art galleries, and even a shoe store, offering many different styles of sneakers, sandals, and flip-flops, with nary a pair of high heels visible in its front window.

That shoe store, Van's, has been owned and operated by the Vanderwerp family for many years. Bill Vanderwerp, the grandson of the store's founder, had just recently taken over operation of the business. Like his father, Bill had also become a drop-in member of the coffee club.

When I got to the bank, I was only semisurprised to find Bill Vanderwerp falling in line behind me.

"Hi, Lee," he said. "I guess you heard about that deputy, Paige."

"Heard what? She was at the hospital after Watt was hurt. I hadn't heard anything today."

"I hear that she didn't show up for work this morning."

"Strange. Does the sheriff have any idea what's up?"

Bill shrugged. "I heard that he didn't seem too surprised."

"Odder and odder."

After I deposited the money, I quickly left the bank, my head swirling with the news.

When I got back to the office, I tried to call Hogan to see if he knew anything more. He wasn't at the station; the secretary took a message.

Before I could even consider getting back to work, Bill Vanderwerp appeared in the shop. I waved at him. He bought half a pound of miniature animals, and before he headed back to the shoe store, he came into my office and plunked himself into my visitor's chair.

"What can I do for you?" I asked.

"There was one other thing I intended to ask you at the bank. But you made a quick getaway."

"Oh, what is it?"

"I can't help wondering if you and Joe have heard anything about these break-ins. Nothing like this ever happened when I was growing up here!" Bill said.

"I don't remember anything like it either," I said. "Of course, I'm a newcomer. I've only been here five years!"

"What do you think of Mike Westerly?"

"He seems very conscientious." I smiled. "And my pal Dolly seems to like him a lot."

"I guess I'm just jumpy. Now that I'm a 'local' again, I find I'm quite protective of the old hometown. I don't trust strangers."

"No matter how long they've been here?"

"Or how recently they arrived."

We both laughed. I'd heard that Bill had worked in New York City for twenty years, so he'd been away from Warner Pier longer than he'd lived in the place.

He smiled, told me how beautiful Aunt Nettie's chocolate animals were, and left.

But the questions about Mike Westerly started to worry me. Who was he? Was he good enough for Dolly? Was his background clean? He seemed like such a nice guy; had the people of Warner Pier—Joe, me, all the others who liked him and trusted him—been taken in and fooled by a stranger?

And what about Watt? Was he an outdoorsman? Or a cook? Or both?

Chapter 10

Was I being disloyal? Or sensible? I didn't know. And I certainly wasn't going to discuss Mike with Dolly. I vowed that I'd try to put the entire thing out of my mind.

Instead, I grabbed a half-pound box of chocolates and stowed it away as a gift for Watt. Aunt Nettie and I could drive into Holland the next day and deliver the box. Chocolate can cure anything!

Then I tried to catch up on work, but I quickly stopped when Hogan finally returned my call. Paige, he told me, had been missed when she failed to show up for work that morning.

"I can't tell if Vinton is more worried about her or about her patrol car," he said. "That may sound harsh, but he doesn't really seem worried about her. He admitted to me that she has called in with flimsy excuses in the past, but this is the first time she simply didn't show up. I guess it's not my business. If her boss doesn't seem to think anything bad has happened to her—I don't know what's going on."

I thought a moment, then spoke. "Well, a couple of funny

things happened, Hogan. First, the other day—after our big apology session with Paige—I accidentally overheard something odd."

I described the phone call I had heard Paige making while I was in the ladies' room.

"I'm sorry I got distracted and didn't tell you earlier. But I'd sure love to know who this Bob is. Surely it's not the same one Mike threatened."

"I might have to ask Mike about that," Hogan said. "What else happened?"

"Last night at the hospital Paige acted strange when Mike came in."

I described the way she had screamed, apparently in amazement, when she saw him. "She sounded really shocked, Hogan. Surprised. And she left right after he showed up. Practically ran out. I didn't understand it at all."

"I'll put that on my list," Hogan said. "It could use an explanation."

Hogan hung up then, and I looked at my computer screen, pretending to think about work, while I tried to figure out what was going on. Was Paige in trouble or even danger? Or just shirking her job, as she'd apparently done in the past?

I tried to concentrate on my own work. But it didn't go well. The phone kept ringing, and each call came from someone I needed to talk to, but who then was in no hurry to hang up. They all kept talking and talking. When I finally got them off the line, Aunt Nettie and her chocolate ladies kept bringing me requests that slowed me down—days off to schedule, lists of items to order, and similar small administrative headaches. This was my job, true, but what I really needed to work on was a plan for Christmas sales. By six o'clock I still had not made a dent in that.

Finally I called Joe and told him he was on his own for dinner.

"I've got some cheese crackers here," I said, "not to mention maybe a thousand pounds of chocolate. I'll nibble on that if I get hungry. You can either take yourself somewhere or warm up the last of the meat loaf and heat a can of green beans."

"I could bring you a hamburger."

"I appreciate the thought, Joe, but you know how much I'd rather talk to you than work. I'd better avoid distractions."

"Okay. As long as you keep the back of the shop locked up tight. Promise?"

"I promise. Besides, the counter girls will be here until eight or eight thirty. I'll try to leave when they do."

I grabbed a Diet Coke from the break room, made sure the locks on the alley doors were secure, and settled in. For the rest of the evening, I vowed, I'd ignore the telephone and get my work done while the counter girls, Barbara and Dale, handled the customers and the calls.

Last year, Aunt Nettie and I had indulged ourselves in expanding and remodeling the shop. At that time, I acquired some fancy shades that allowed me to have privacy while I worked. The shades covered the glass interior walls of my office, allowing me to see out, but preventing people on the street and customers from seeing in. Now I lowered them and went to my desk. There I stopped for a moment to enjoy the passing scene outside.

The sun hadn't set yet, and the street was still crowded. Teenagers were walking up and down in groups, flirting. Burly guys were flexing their muscles to display T-shirts with tacky slogans printed on the front. Older women were limping by, likely having developed blisters from their new beach sandals.

Two young women in particular drew my attention; they seemed familiar, but I couldn't remember where I had seen them before. One was blond and the other brunette. Were they customers? Were they among the waitresses at the Sidewalk Café? Or were they simply people who walked up and down the sidewalk now and then? As I watched, the two of them faced our show window, put their hands on either side of their faces, and stuck their tongues out, making faces at Barbara and Dale. Barbara and Dale made faces back, and all four of them laughed.

I joined the chuckles as the two girls waved and walked on down the street.

I called out, "Hey! Who are those girls?"

Dale came to my office door. "They work at the shoe store," she said. "They come in for a bonbon every couple of days. I don't remember how the crazy face game started. We try not to do it in front of customers."

"Please don't! Our customers are crazy enough. But I needed a laugh."

We all giggled, and I went back to work.

The phone stopped ringing after six o'clock, and everything began to go more smoothly. We had enough customers to keep Barbara and Dale busy, but not so many that I had to leave my desk to help them at the display counter. I drank my Diet Coke and ate a small sack of cheese crackers while typing up information for the Christmas sales brochure my assistant, Bunny, was to design for me. I was making great headway.

When Barbara finally stuck her head into the office to tell me she and Dale were ready to leave, I looked up in surprise.

"Yikes!" I said. "I'm nearly through, too. Maybe I should work late every night. I seem to get more done."

Barbara laughed. "I keep telling you that it would be easier to sell chocolate if the customers would quit dropping by to bother you by buying it."

"Yes, if the customers would just stay home . . ."

"And Joe called and ordered Dale and me to walk you out to your van tonight."

"Oh, he did, did he? He ordered you? I thought I was in charge of TenHuis Chocolade. When did Joe start giving the orders?"

"I'm not sure," she said. "But I noticed that your aunt gave you the alley parking spot today."

"That's true."

"So if we all go out the back, you could give Dale and me a ride to the municipal parking lot."

"You're parked there? Well, that municipal lot is kind of far and snaky. It would be a good idea for the three of us to leave together."

"We can wait until you're ready."

"I'm nearly ready. I'll just grab my stuff."

I closed out my computer and gathered up my belongings, saying, "Tomorrow our new security system is going to be installed."

Barbara grinned at me. "Hopefully, that'll mean the end of the concern about break-ins for us."

"And maybe the start of a lot of false alarms, too, until we get used to it. But the salesman promised the new equipment is simple to operate."

I put on my light jacket and dug my purse out of my desk.

I pulled my handheld alarm, car keys, and flashlight out of the purse, and I stuck them in the jacket pockets, where they'd be easy to grab if I needed them. I turned out most of the indoor lights, turned on the alley's security lights, and headed for the back door. Dale and Barbara followed me.

I had just taken out the keys to the alley door when the screaming started.

At first I wasn't frightened. Just startled. Then Dale grabbed my arm. I could see her lips move, but the screaming drowned out most of what she was saying.

"Someone's being attacked!"

Dale was right. I pointed to the telephone. "Call 9-1-1! I'll see what's going on out back!"

Someone was now pounding on the alley door. I threw the lock, yanked the door open, and plunged outside.

The screaming grew frantic. "Help! Help!" I saw that two young women were huddling on our small back porch. Another door—the one to Dolly's apartment—flew open as if it had exploded. Dolly leaped onto the porch, holding a golf club over her head. She yelled something I couldn't understand.

At the sight of Dolly waving a golf club, the two girls screamed even louder.

"Get inside!" I yelled over the noise and motioned them past me. I'm sure no one heard me, though they seemed to understand. I grabbed one of the girls and shoved her inside our back door. Dolly grabbed the second one and shoved her inside. Then Dolly and I stood shoulder to shoulder in the doorway, looking around.

The alley was mostly black, with pools of light from a few security lights.

"Is anybody there?" Dolly yelled.

"Do you see anybody?" As I spoke, a loud clang echoed down the alley. Dolly and I both whirled toward the sound.

"Somebody's moving down toward Dock Street!" Dolly jumped down the porch steps, almost tumbling over the raccoon cage, and ran to her left.

"Wait!" I stumbled after her. I could see a vague outline of figures moving against the glare of Dock Street.

"Slow down, Dolly! We can't just follow some strangers down a dark alley!"

Dolly was far ahead of me by that time. I had to chase her down and grab her arm before she would slow down. Then she dragged me along for several steps.

"Dolly! They could be armed!"

Finally we came to a stop, and I realized she had a flashlight, one of those big suckers. I dug out my own flashlight, but it was too small to spotlight the people we were chasing. I stuck my other hand into my jacket pocket, ready to sound my alarm.

I could hear feet pounding, moving away from us toward Dock Street. Lights were dancing along; the runners had pulled out their own flashlights.

Dolly yelled. "There they go!"

She took off toward their bouncing lights, pulling me along. We ran down the alley until we reached Dock Street. Then we skidded to a halt, and Dolly dropped the aim of her giant flash toward the pavement. We no longer needed a spotlight to recognize people.

Dock Street was curved, following the banks of the Warner River, a block away from us. We stood on the sidewalk, looking to the left, then to the right, hoping to see something suspicious.

But all we saw were the ordinary sights of Dock Street on a summer evening—the streetlights, the park across the street, and Herrera's Restaurant catty-corner from us. Bill Vanderwerp was entering its door, just the way he did most evenings. Tourists, their ice cream cones dripping, were walking down the street. The display windows were brightly lit.

After a moment, I spoke. "What the heck are we looking for?"

"Darned if I know!"

"Did you see anybody, Dolly?"

"No! For a moment, maybe. But mainly I just heard the yelling and saw figures moving!"

I fought a desire to laugh. "I guess we'd better go back."

We retreated down the alley until we reached the back door of TenHuis Chocolade. I felt pretty stupid, and I think Dolly did, too.

"What happened?" I said. "What was all that yelling about?"

"I sure don't know, but it sounded like an emergency!"

At that point, I heard sirens, and within seconds, two Warner Pier patrol cars wheeled into the other end of the alley.

Dolly turned toward me, and I read her lips. "Yikes!" she said.

"That's what I say," I said. "Double yikes!"

Ten minutes later, two patrol officers were searching the alley while six women—Dolly, Barbara, Dale, the two girls who had screamed, and me—were sitting in our shop's break room feeling like idiots. Or at least that's how I felt.

I turned to the two newcomers. By then, I had recognized them. They were the two who had made faces at Barbara and Dale through our front window.

"You two work at Van's Shoes, don't you?" I said.

They nodded like bobbleheads, the brunette head and the blond head moving in unison, their eyes still big and round.

Both were tiny—petite little things. Both looked to be around twenty. Maybe even eighteen or nineteen. They wore tight skirts and T-shirts, and their cute sandals were embellished with beads. In other words, they looked like typical Warner Pier working girls—young women who held jobs in a tourist town.

"What were y'all doing in the alley?" I asked.

The dark-haired one spoke first. "Trying to get away!"

"Someone came out of the garage," the other said. They explained that as part of their pay at the shoe shop, they were allowed to live in an apartment across the alley from Van's Shoes.

"Bill Vanderwerp owns the building," the blonde girl continued. "There's an office downstairs, and we live upstairs. The garage goes with the apartment. But neither of us has a car. We get to work by just walking across the alley."

The blond girl identified herself as Katy, and the dark-haired one as Darcy. The two had been working alone at Van's Shoes that night. The shoe shop closed at seven, and after locking up, the two of them had gone for sandwiches at the drugstore.

"We were trying to cheer ourselves up," Darcy said. "Someone we know has gone missing."

"Paige?" I asked.

They nodded.

"Do you know her well?" I asked.

"Not really. But she lives in Dorinda, where we're from, and she helped us get our jobs at Van's."

Tears welled up in Darcy's eyes. "She's a lot older than we are—practically thirty—but she's been really nice. Never treats us like little kids. And her boss doesn't seem to be worried about her at all!"

Because Katy and Darcy had closed the shop for the day, the shoe store had been empty. But as the two girls came back to their apartment, the garage door under it opened, and two big, lumpy figures stepped out.

Darcy and Katy reacted exactly the way many residents had been reacting to anything unexpected since the mysterious break-ins began. They screamed like banshees and took off down the alley.

"We saw your light come on," Katy said. "So we thought there was someone here."

That's when Dolly and I had joined the fray, shoving the two girls into the shop and running down the alley after the vague figures. Then the sirens had joined us.

By the time everything settled down, Bill Vanderwerp had been called to check on his store. The sheriff's deputies were waiting for him to arrive, and they had joined our group, huddled around Darcy and Katy.

"Can you describe the people you saw?" one of the deputies asked.

"They were great, big blobs," Katy said. "I didn't wait around to get a good look."

The deputy sighed. "It sure would have been helpful if you had. You say Mrs. Woodyard had just turned on the lights in the alley. And if the unknown person ran toward Dock Street, he—or she—must have run right past you."

"Behind us, maybe!" Darcy's voice was still trembling. "I sure didn't look around. I was trying to claw the door to the chocolate shop open—even if it was locked."

"But you feel sure the figures were coming out of the garage?"

Katy and Darcy did their simultaneous nodding act again.

I jumped into the conversation at that point, turning to the deputy. "Have you looked in the garage?"

"We're waiting for Bill Vanderwerp to bring a key," the deputy said.

"Oh!" Darcy reached into her pocket. "I have a key," she said. "I didn't realize you needed to get in there."

Silence fell over our little group. *Well, duh.*

"I'm sorry," Darcy said. "I guess I'm rattled." She handed the deputy a key ring, pointing out the garage key.

I felt pretty dumb about the whole thing, too. The girls had told us the garage went with their apartment, but when they said they didn't use it, I'd assumed they gave up the key. Duh, to me!

The deputy took the garage key and went out our back door. "Let me through," he said, weaving a path through the half-dozen law officers, including the sheriff, who were standing between him and the garage.

Vinton took the key, and the law officers all closed in behind him as he leaned over in front of the lock. We heard clicks as the lock turned.

I decided to stay on our porch. That was where the best view would be. Dolly and I stood shoulder to shoulder on the top step. The sound of muttering came from the group of lawmen, and I heard sentences. "Where's the light switch?" "Try the wall." "Is there a pull chain?"

It was too dark to see what was inside the garage, even from the vantage point of the top porch step. But whatever was inside was big and white.

Dolly grabbed my arm and spoke in a harsh whisper. "There's a vehicle in there."

I nodded.

Then the overhead light flashed on, giving us a fairly good view of what was inside. And in the silence that followed we saw a white SUV with the word SHERIFF in big black letters across the back.

It was a patrol car bearing the insignia of the Warner County Sheriff's Department.

"Oh no!" I don't know who said it.

That was the last thing anyone said as Sheriff Vinton edged alongside the car and opened the driver's side door. We all watched silently as he caught the body that fell out. I think it was Vinton who finally spoke.

"Damn! I thought she'd gone off on a toot again!"

Chapter 11

Perhaps it's understandable that the rest of the evening is a blur to me.

Mike arrived shortly after Paige's body was discovered. He sat with us and held Dolly's hand, softly talking in her ear. I remember she kept shaking her head, and he kept nodding his. But they were not disagreeing.

Joe and Hogan came later, showing up forty-five minutes after the garage door opened. They'd been having dinner together in Holland, and the dispatcher tracked them down. Hogan huddled with Mike and Dolly, then with Vinton. Joe stayed with me, then scurried over to the group clustered around Hogan. Back and forth.

Until they got there, Dolly and I had to be the adults. We were the ones who had to find the parents of Katy and Darcy and ask them to pick up the tearful girls and take them home to Dorinda. We had to make sure Barbara and Dale got home safely. We had to talk to Bill Vanderwerp calmly. Bill appeared understandably stunned that a young woman had been found dead on his property.

"I can't believe this," Bill said. "The only time I met Paige was when she came over about some shoplifting case."

That confused me a bit. "Darcy and Katy said she helped them get jobs at your shop," I said.

Bill shrugged. "I had printed up a flyer about summer jobs," he said. "Maybe Paige picked one up and gave it to the girls."

Paige's family now lived in northeastern Michigan, we learned. Vinton got the responsibility of calling them.

At least I didn't have to do that chore. I was already feeling pretty bad because I hadn't liked Paige, and now she had apparently committed suicide.

I told Joe as much. "I guess I feel guilty," I said.

"Don't be silly," he said. "If everybody I don't like committed suicide, the streets would be piled with corpses. And I like a lot more people than I dislike! You're not responsible for other people's problems."

I looked at him closely. "Then you think Paige committed suicide?"

Joe didn't answer.

As soon as we settled the younger generation—Barbara, Dale, Katy, and Darcy—Joe told me it was time for me to leave, too. I didn't argue. We went home. And never had the old white farmhouse looked so good. We didn't talk about the whole thing anymore that night.

But the next morning I was up and dressed early—which was a good thing, as it turned out, because Hogan showed up at seven thirty.

Joe didn't seem surprised to see Hogan. He went to the back door and waved as the chief's car pulled into the drive. Then Joe turned to me.

"Hogan told me last night that he was going to drop by. Could you stand to talk to him?"

"As long as I don't have to make sense. What does he want?"

"Just something about those raccoons."

"Raccoons! Now what? I'd like to forget all about raccoons for today."

Joe brought me a cup of coffee, accompanied by three chocolate animals: a dark chocolate raccoon, a white chocolate rabbit, and a milk chocolate squirrel. Yes, chocolate is wonderful for breakfast.

After Hogan sat down with us and his own coffee, Joe spoke. "Hogan and I would like to have your opinion on a couple of things he and I talked about over dinner yesterday evening."

I sipped my coffee. "Oh? What did you need to know, Hogan?"

"Well, I did wonder if you had time to talk to Wildflower Hill."

"About Watt? Actually I did. I'm afraid I didn't learn much."

"Nothing?"

"She thinks Watt came from 'up north, maybe on the U.P.' She doesn't know anything else about him, really. Except that she likes him. Oh, and maybe he'd been in the army. Were you able to find out anything?"

"Not a lot. I got in touch with Mike Herrera, who says Watt was pleasant, reliable, and a good cook. He worked for his restaurants just that one summer, so Mike remembered only a few personal things about Watt. I checked state records—nothing there."

I realized that Hogan was saying Watt had no criminal record in Michigan, something I'd already guessed.

Hogan shrugged. "I'll do a little more checking. But what happened last night? From your viewpoint, I mean."

My voice cracked when I tried to answer. I struggled not to break down. Joe patted my back and assured me that I was an intelligent and capable woman and that he had every confidence in me. He held my hand while I again told the tale of what happened the night before. Ending with the discovery of Paige's body in the garage.

Hogan listened with a frown, and he kept frowning after I finished.

"So I guess she committed suicide," I said. "But it's hard to believe."

"Why do you say that, Lee? You barely knew Paige."

I considered for a time. "First, it was the 'big, lumpy' figures Darcy and Katy saw."

Hogan frowned. "If they saw anything at all."

"Something scared the girls, Hogan. They ran. Plus, I guess it was one of the things Paige said when I was eavesdropping. Something about being on the edge of—some big deal? That's not right—it was 'historic'! She said something about 'on the edge of a historic deal.' That was it."

Hogan sat up and stared at me. He looked surprised. But he didn't speak.

So I did. "I just can't believe someone 'on the edge of a historic deal' would commit suicide."

Hogan frowned. "I don't understand that either," he said. "But there's another thing. Both you and Dolly mentioned a noise I don't understand. A clanging noise. What was that?"

"I have no idea, Hogan. We didn't stop to figure it out."

"Did it sound familiar in any way?"

"It was metallic. It was loud. It reverberated. Clanged."

Hogan was still frowning, so I asked his opinion. "I'm sure you and your gang looked the alley over in detail. Did you see anything likely to clang?"

"Garbage can lids," he said. "There are several big Dumpsters. But the only things I found unusual in any of them were some moving pads. I'll take another look."

"Do you think something is—well, wrong about the whole deal? Something that doesn't sound like suicide?"

"It's hard to tell, Lee. I'd like to understand that noise, and I'd like to understand those big, bulky guys coming out of the garage. At the very least, they could be witnesses. But did they really come out of the garage where Paige was? Could the girls have been mistaken? Could they have come from somewhere else?"

"I didn't see where they came from. They were already running toward Dock Street when I saw them. Ask Dolly. She had a better view."

"I've talked to the state police. They're recommending leaving the status of Paige's death open."

"Open?"

"Not declaring a cause of death. Meanwhile, Joe had a revelation."

A revelation? What else could have been going on? I turned to Joe. "So?"

"This was a different idea of just what happened," Joe said. "I'd like to ask if you agree with me."

"Ask away."

Joe sat forward. "To begin, nearly a week ago, Wildflower recommended Watt Wicker as a raccoon catcher. Agreed?"

"Yes. I called him that night, and we talked about the job."

Joe nodded. "Early the next morning, Mike Westerly was with the coffee club in the Rest-Stop, and that's when Mike told me he would be glad to try catching raccoons for you."

I frowned. "You told me that. But I didn't need a raccoon catcher by then. I'd hired Watt to handle the job."

"Right. But I didn't know that at the time. I told Mike—and not only Mike, but also the entire coffee club—that it was likely you would accept his offer to trap raccoons at TenHuis Chocolade."

"But I *didn't* hire Mike, because I'd already hired Watt."

"True. I was mistaken."

This confession seemed trivial. I smiled as I replied. "Joe, I think you're overreacting to having two raccoon hunters on the job at the same time. Mike was just being nice to me. He didn't care about the raccoons."

Joe nodded. "True. But no one at the Rest-Stop knew Watt was going to be the raccoon hunter. They were expecting Mike to show up. And unless *you* told somebody, nobody knew the situation had changed."

"So what?"

"So did Watt nearly get killed because he was where Mike was expected to be?"

I stared at Joe. My mouth fell open.

I jumped up off the couch so fast that I nearly landed on my knees. "Oh my gosh, Joe! Are you saying somebody attacked Watt thinking he was Mike?"

"Maybe not—"

"Joe, they might try again! We can't let Mike wander around

with someone out there trying to murder him, and we can't let these crooks get away with hurting Watt!"

Joe tried to soothe me. "Lee! Lee!" he said, speaking as if I were a child.

"Joe!" I was ready to pop a gasket. "Joe, we've got to do something!"

Now I had Hogan as well as Joe soothing me. "It's all right," he said. "We've got it temporarily handled."

"What? What did you do?"

"I fired Mike." Hogan grinned. "I told him he should take some time away from Warner Pier."

"Really?" I felt completely incredulous. "That's not a good solution either!"

"Calm down, Lee. Mike will get his job back. This is just a stopgap measure. We're simply trying to keep Mike out of the firing line."

"I hope he'll go."

"I'm bribing him. I told him to take Dolly with him."

"But that will put Dolly in danger!"

Hogan was frowning. "I'm afraid she may already be in danger, Lee. She was the one who got closest to the 'big, lumpy' guys when they came out of the garage. I think it's probably a good thing for her to keep a low profile for a while."

I dropped my head into my hands and shook that head gently. "I don't want to see Dolly in danger."

"She probably isn't. But I want to take every precaution."

"I only hope both of them will go," I said. "And that the Cookie Monsters don't discover where."

"I'm not saying where they are," Hogan said. "But it's someplace safe. And just in case, Watt is in a safe place, too."

"Thank goodness! Are you telling where he is?"

"Nope."

I nodded in approval.

Eventually, the three of us settled down, and I got a full report on Joe and Hogan's evening.

It started with dinner. Since I was working late and Aunt Nettie had gone to the bridal shower for a friend's granddaughter, Joe and Hogan decided to go into Holland for dinner together. There, they fell into a conversation about the urban raccoons around Warner Pier.

Joe had mentioned Mike's offer to trap raccoons behind TenHuis Chocolade and explained how Watt ended up taking the job instead.

And the light dawned. He wondered aloud if anyone but Mike had known that I rejected his offer to trap the varmints. Joe and Hogan quickly realized the possibility that Mike had been the intended victim of the attack in the dark alley—not Watt.

They got to work without hesitation. Joe called all the coffee club members and asked if any of them had told anyone about Mike and Watt both being considered as raccoon trappers. They all denied that they had.

"But, Joe," I said, "there were other people who knew."

"Who?"

"Me, for one. Alex Gold. Aunt Nettie."

"She said she didn't tell anyone," Joe said. "We'll have to ask Alex if he did."

"I know one other person who might have," I said. "T. J."

Hogan nodded. "I've been trying to reach T. J. He's supposed to call when he wakes up. He's planning to work tonight."

I was surprised. "This soon after his coworker was attacked?"

"His mom says he told her he didn't mind, as long as he had someone to work with him. She found a tough guy to stand in for Watt—T. J.'s dad."

Joe laughed. "Tony used to get all the worst jobs in his father's restaurants, but I doubt he remembers a lot about cleaning grease traps."

Ten minutes later, T. J. called. Hogan put his phone on speaker so all three of us could hear, then began to ask questions.

"T. J., I need to talk to you about Watt. Did you know he was going to be catching raccoons for Lee and Nettie? Before he did it, I mean?"

"I sure didn't, Chief. Not until he mentioned it the first night he was on the job."

"No discussion about it at all?"

"No, sir."

"Frankly, T. J., it would help our case if you *had* known and then told someone."

"Then I wish I could tell you that I had. But I didn't."

T. J. said good-bye then, and Hogan, Joe, and I sat silently.

"There's always a possibility that someone made some casual comment," I said. "This is Warner Pier, remember. News seems to seep out by osmosis. In fact, there's no reason that Watt couldn't have told somebody himself."

Both Joe and Hogan shook their heads.

"Didn't you hear?" Hogan said. "Watt regained full consciousness yesterday afternoon. And he told me he hadn't mentioned this particular raccoon-catching job to anybody."

My head was spinning. When Hogan's phone rang again, it seemed to echo between my ears.

But I was surprised when Hogan jumped to his feet. "Mike! Is everything okay?"

He listened silently for a moment before he spoke again. "Where did she go?" It had to be Dolly. My eyes widened.

Another moment of silence. "Did she leave a note?"

Next. "That's no help. Do you have *any* idea where she is?"

Then. "No! No, Mike, let me think a minute."

Hogan stalked around the living room, his cell phone to his ear. "No, don't come back. We'd better stick to our original plan—at least for today. I'll call you as soon as I find anything out." He shot a glance toward Joe and me as he listened, nodding. "Good. So go to the place we agreed on. And stay there."

He sighed. "And, Mike, remember. Strictly incommunicado."

Hogan looked like a thundercloud as he hung up. Neither Joe nor I spoke.

"It's Dolly," Hogan said. "After we made our big plan, she's changed it. She's disappeared from her apartment. When Mike went to pick her up, she was gone."

I jumped to my feet. "Gone! Gone? Mike doesn't know where she went?"

"She left a note, but all it says is 'Don't worry. I'm okay.'"

Chapter 12

I wanted to shake her—if I'd only been able to get my hands on her.

"Dolly's the one who needs to worry! First she agrees to hide out with Mike, then she backs out and tells us not to worry? What does she *think* we're all going to do?"

I was furious. Where would Dolly have gone? Had she left on her own? Or was she forced to go away with someone? Could she have been kidnapped? But if she left a note—well, did that mean she went willingly? Or that someone had forced her to write the note?

Joe asked the logical question. "Exactly what did the note say?"

"It says she isn't unhappy about leaving," Hogan said. "She simply felt she couldn't hide out with Mike. So she's gone, but she promised to get in touch."

Naturally, my first idea was to call Dolly's cell phone. All I got were instructions to leave a message. A try at sending her an e-mail was equally unsuccessful; she didn't answer. This did not reassure me. I worried all day.

I worried and agonized and pulled my hair and chewed my nails and worried some more. That was all I could do; Hogan wouldn't allow either Joe or me to do anything else, such as get out and look for her.

No. He said it firmly. Dolly had left a note. There was no reason to think she was in danger. But the whole plan had been for Mike and Dolly to leave town together. If her friends rushed around, making noise about her disappearing, it might raise suspicions about Mike's whereabouts. No, we must keep this a secret.

Joe and I had worked with Hogan on a number of cases—his force was tiny, and he called on volunteers when he needed help. But we understood that he was in charge. Our situation was nothing like one of those mystery stories with an idiot professional detective who had to be led along by the amateurs. No, Hogan was the boss.

So I understood what he was saying, but I hated doing nothing. I was ready to spend the whole day on the phone, calling all of Dolly's friends and relatives to find out if she had turned up on anyone's doorstep. I wanted to plaster the television and radio news shows with alerts about a missing woman, patrol the streets in police cars with loud sirens, and send up flares.

I dragged myself into work a couple of hours late. Aunt Nettie met me there, as tired and worried about Dolly as I was. At least she brought doughnuts; Aunt Nettie never forgets the comfort food.

When she and I discovered a big box of homemade cookies in the break room, with a note from Dolly taped on top, we both cried.

"Please eat these," the note said. "I don't want them to get stale."

After we got the tears over, we washed our faces, refreshed our makeup, and put on smiles so that all the ladies who made our wonderful chocolate would not guess there was anything wrong. We practiced saying that Dolly had taken a day off for personal business.

But the first phone call of the day was a supplier asking for Dolly, and it nearly knocked me flat. How could I answer in a pleasant voice, "She's not here today. May I help you?" But I managed to do it.

The morning crawled along, and when twelve o'clock finally rolled around, Hogan took Aunt Nettie and me to lunch. He reassured us that Dolly had gone—wherever—of her own volition.

As we came back from picking at our lunch, I saw a gorgeous silver Corvette parked a few slots down from us in our alley.

My mood lifted, and I crowed. "Alex! He's back!"

"You go check on him," Aunt Nettie said. "I'll finish packing the March's order and go down to say hi to Alex later."

I ran next door and pounded on the back door of Alex Gold's jewelry shop. In a few seconds, our neighbor—both at home and in downtown Warner Pier—opened his door and invited me in.

"I'm so glad to see you," I said. "And you look just fine. As if nothing had happened."

"I feel fine, too," Alex said. "Once I got Garnet to stop hovering over me, it was as if nothing had happened. I still don't understand why on earth these crooks don't take anything! It's not good for my reputation as a jeweler if I'm not wearing anything a burglar thinks is worth stealing! But come on in. I want to show you my new security system."

The security system was impressive—much like the one Aunt Nettie and I were to have installed later that day.

"Have you tested it?" I asked.

"Here, I'll set the back-door alarm, and you can test it."

I laughed. "We'll have the cops here in a minute!"

"I'll call the company and tell them we're testing it."

Alex made his call, and I tried to open the back door. In a second, a piercing alarm stabbed my ears. I hastily stuck my fingers in them, and Alex tapped a code into the panel near the door. Silence fell immediately.

The noise was certainly effective. Alex had pasted sheets of brown paper over the front windows, but I could tell by the shadows against the glass that passersby were stopping to see what had caused the din.

"That ought to scare off an intruder," Alex said.

"That'll send them running for the hills," I agreed. "I only hope our system works as well."

Alex leaned toward me and lowered his voice. "Did you ever wonder if these break-ins are secretly orchestrated by alarm companies?"

"Huh?"

"Sure. Look how many systems they're selling because all the Warner Pier merchants are scared out of their khakis over these intruders."

We laughed. Then Alex showed me around the shop and explained where everything would go. He pointed out the display cases, the hidden cameras, the office with a one-way window overlooking the sales room, and the safe, where a lot of the stock would be tucked away each evening. A nook with a small table would allow customers to sit down and try on items they were drooling over.

The color scheme was black-and-white. "It's got to suit both modern items and antiques," Alex said.

"And engagement rings?" I asked.

"Of course. It's not a jewelry store without engagement rings. But our emphasis will be antique and handmade jewelry. Some of it will be—well, folksy. It will have a handcrafted look."

I saw that Alex had been eating his own lunch in the back room. A colorful book with beautiful photographs of showy jewelry sat in front of his carton of yogurt.

I pointed to it. "I see you think about jewelry even during meals."

Alex laughed, but the sound seemed a bit forced. "I'm a fifth-generation jeweler, Lee. Our blood runs ruby red."

He reached over and picked up a small bag of potato chips with one hand, then closed the book with the other. Then he dropped the chips, which somehow managed to land on the title of the book.

Then he looked at me rather slyly. For a moment I felt that I'd surprised Alex looking at dirty pictures, not beautiful jewels.

I swallowed a giggle as I said good-bye and headed to the back door. Alex promised to set the new alarm system while he was in the building alone.

"Even though there's nothing valuable here now," he said.

"You're here! None of us could get along without you."

I said good-bye and left through the back door. I pondered the Gold family as I walked back to the shop. Alex's mother had been the famed opera singer Opal Diamonte. She married a well-to-do jeweler named Reuben Gold. Since *Rubin* means "ruby" in German, and *diamante* translates from Italian as "diamond," they each had two names that were similar to precious stones or precious metals. This inspired the Golds to name their children after jewels—Ruby, Pearl, and Alexandrite, which was Alex's full name. Alex also had two nieces, Garnet and Jade.

But Garnet, our neighbor across Lake Shore Drive, and her sister, Jade, had declared an end to the jewel names. Garnet's children were named Mary and Richard Junior, and Jade's daughters were Carol and Beth.

The Gold family's unusual names brought my thoughts back to Dolly Jolly, who had a sister named Molly. Despite a lot of good-natured teasing, they denied that they had an aunt named Polly or a brother named Wally.

That thought made me smile, but also brought a tear to my eye. Where was Dolly? She was my friend, and I missed her. And I was terribly worried about her, even if she claimed to be perfectly safe.

I swallowed my worry and went through the back door of TenHuis Chocolade. I was immediately waylaid by Aunt Nettie, who whispered in my ear, "Look at your e-mail! Quick!"

The first item was from Dolly.

Aunt Nettie and I hugged each other enthusiastically, even though the e-mail was merely a copy of an order sent to our nut supplier. Wherever she was, Dolly was on the job.

I whispered, "Oh, Aunt Nettie! I feel so much better."

I tried again to e-mail and text Dolly, but she didn't answer. Still, wherever she was, she was working. This discovery helped me feel ready to meet the installer from the security company a half hour later.

The installer worked efficiently, walking around the shop with Aunt Nettie and me, describing what he could install to make our doors and windows safe from intruders. He also checked our fire alarms. Then he produced a tool kit, and in less than an hour, we were all set up with a sophisticated alarm system.

I was impressed and admitted it out loud. "This is great!"

The installer smiled. "I hope you never need it. But if you ever do, it will call the police and our regional office."

As he left, Aunt Nettie presented him with a half-pound box of strawberry truffles ("white chocolate interior enrobed in dark chocolate and decorated with dark chocolate sprinkles") and mocha pyramids ("milky coffee interior inside a dark chocolate pyramid").

"I'm surprised at how much more secure I feel already," I said.

"I feel secure, too," Aunt Nettie said. "And it didn't take long."

Then I laughed. "We'll be safe from intruders, but not from raccoons," I said. "An electronic system won't help a bit with stopping them. And with Watt Wicker still out, that project has come to a standstill."

Aunt Nettie sighed. "I hate to replace Watt after he was injured. I'll call Hogan and ask what his status is. I meant to ask at lunch."

In a few minutes she came into my office. She was frowning.

"I talked to Hogan," she said. "And it seems that Watt is out of pocket, too."

"What?! Like Dolly?"

"No. No, Hogan thinks Watt simply wandered away from where Mike and Hogan had hidden him. There's no reason to think he's in danger, but they don't know where he is."

"Can I help search for him?"

"Hogan says no. He's got Mike back in his hiding place and wants him to stay there. I think he feels that Watt is simply wandering and will turn up. Then they'll find a better hiding place."

She gave me a pat on the back. "Lee, you seem awfully tired. Why don't you go home?"

"It's only four o'clock."

"But you came in an hour early."

She was right, and I agreed that I'd had such a bad night the previous night that I was ready to take a hot shower, eat a cheese sandwich and some tomato soup, and hit the rack.

I kissed Aunt Nettie on the cheek. "And I recommend that you do the same thing."

"I might," she said. "I could leave Bunny in charge."

"She can handle it until closing. I'll go over the new lockup rules with her."

I was still parking at the municipal lot, since Watt's raccoon trap was taking my parking space. After I talked to Bunny, I gathered my belongings and headed out the front door. I was absolutely exhausted, and I still had to walk uphill for four blocks to get to my car.

I'll swear I fell asleep at Warner Pier's one stoplight as I left town. But I made it out to Lake Shore Drive to our lane, stopped to pick up the mail, then parked the van in my usual spot in the drive. The click of the key in the back door's lock sounded like the door to heaven opening, and I quietly went inside.

I walked into the dining room, stood by the table, and started sorting the mail. As usual, it was mostly junk.

I had just reached the third charity donation request when the upstairs shower came on.

Cheese for Fudge?

(The Chocolate Falcon Fraud)

Nearly every summer I visit the Mystery Readers Book Club at the Herrick District Library in Holland, Michigan. At one of the meetings, member Carrie Stroh mentioned that she always used a recipe for fudge that called for Velveeta cheese. The recipe came from her mother. Intrigued, to say the least, I knew I had to try it.

Velveeta Cheese Fudge

1 pound margarine or butter
1 pound Velveeta
1 cup cocoa
4 pounds powdered sugar
1 tablespoon vanilla

Melt together 1 pound of margarine or butter and 1 pound of Velveeta.

Sift together 1 cup cocoa and 4 pounds of powdered sugar. (That's a *lot* of powdered sugar. Use the biggest bowl in the kitchen.)

Mix the sifted cocoa and sugar thoroughly, then add the melted butter and cheese. Add 1 tablespoon vanilla. (I added the vanilla to the butter and cheese first.)

Carrie says, "Stir, stir, stir until your hand cramps. Spread evenly in a buttered 9-inch-by-13-inch pan. Cool and cut into squares."

I interpreted "Stir, stir, stir" as "beat," as with traditional fudge. But when I first made the recipe, I discovered that mixing the cheese-butter mixture with the sugar-cocoa mixture is a Job with a capital *J*. It's extremely stiff. Beating this would be impossible. But the resulting fudge is perfectly smooth and absolutely delicious.

Chapter 13

Talk about being startled.

My first impulse was to run out the back door, climb into my van, and back out of the drive, steering with my left hand and calling 9-1-1 with my right.

But I stopped to think. What the heck kind of an intruder would break in to take a shower?

That made no sense at all. Except once our neighbor's house had been entered by a homeless person who didn't otherwise have access to a shower. In our neighborhood, just a mile off the interstate with its attraction to hitchhikers, that could happen. But it usually happened in the winter, when homeless people needed warm places. Currently, the weather was great; I wouldn't expect people needing shelter to break into houses. And if they felt dirty, they could take a swim in Lake Michigan.

And it wasn't likely that the person in the shower was Joe. He might have come home and decided to take a shower, but he wouldn't use the upstairs shower instead of the one downstairs, adjoining our bedroom. Besides, his truck wasn't there, at our house.

A friend? Did we know anyone who might drop by and decide to take a shower? Unlikely.

A relative? That seemed too odd even for our oddest relatives. And how would a friend or relative get in? Only a few of them had keys, and a quick circuit of the downstairs revealed that all the doors and windows were properly locked.

I could still hear the shower running as I decided to leave. I had exhausted the possibilities of people who might legitimately be taking a shower.

I grabbed my purse and ran out the kitchen door, headed for my van. I was opening its door before I noticed that the side door of the garage was firmly closed. I skidded to a stop. That door is usually slightly ajar; we have to slam it hard to get it to fit.

Our "garage" actually functions as a storage shed. The little building was built as a garage, true. But that was in the 1930s, when cars—and therefore garages—were much smaller than today. Neither my van, which doubles as a delivery truck for Ten-Huis Chocolade, nor Joe's truck, which is big enough to haul an extra-long boat, would fit into that garage. We use the building to store things like yard furniture or picnic supplies. None of it is valuable, and we're careless about closing it firmly.

Breaking into our house to take a shower was odd; breaking into a garage filled with hoes, rakes, and lawn chairs was even odder.

I changed the direction of my flight from my van to that door. I threw the door open and reached inside to turn on the light.

Inside was a red Volkswagen. Not an antique-ish one left

over from the '50s or '60s. This one was bright, new—one of the final Beetles made. And I knew who owned it.

"Aha!" I believe I shouted, then I whirled and rushed back into the house. The shower was no longer running. I ran up the stairs, ignoring the amount of noise I was making, and I banged on the bathroom door.

"Dolly! Dolly!" I yelled the name. "What the heck are you doing here?"

The door flew open, and I was facing a giant with wild red hair sticking up in all directions. She had a huge blue towel draped around her as a sarong.

"Lee!" she boomed out. "What are you doing home this early? I thought I could get a shower and be all ready to surprise you!"

"We've been so worried! Where have you been all day?"

"I drove into Holland and went to a motel! I registered under my mother's name. I had her credit card because I'd been doing some shopping for her. Then I decided it would be more fun to ask you and Joe to take me in!"

"I'd hug you if you weren't so darn wet!"

"Give me ten minutes, and I'll be downstairs!" As usual, Dolly's voice rumbled like thunder echoing over the lake.

"If I weren't so glad to see you, I'd bawl you out," I said.

"Be sure you pull the curtains! I don't want your neighbors to know I'm here!"

By the time Dolly came downstairs—dressed in jeans and a T-shirt, with dry hair—I had made iced tea. When I poured her a glass, she snatched it up and took a big slurp.

"I tried to do some work today," she said.

"We got at least one e-mail. It gave Aunt Nettie and me hope that you were okay. Your note was vague."

"When I wrote that note, my hideout plan was vague," Dolly said.

"I've closed the dining room curtains. Let's sit in there, and you can Tell All." I shook a finger at her. "But you'll have to whisper, Dolly. In case one of the neighbors walks up to the back door. We've done enough yelling."

We sat down with our iced tea and Dolly began her report.

As I had already been told, during their talk the previous evening Joe and Hogan had concluded that Mike had been the possible target of the attack that had injured Watt. They had been calling members of the coffee club to ask about this when I called and told them Paige's body had been discovered. Their continued discussion—as they drove back to Warner Pier—had convinced them that there was a serious possibility the two events were connected.

Plus, as Hogan heard more about the discovery of Paige's body, he began to fear that Dolly had been seen by the two "lumpy" people who had been near the garage where Paige was found.

So before Joe and Hogan arrived on the scene in our alley, the two of them tracked Mike down by phone and urged him to hide out and stay hidden from whoever had injured Watt. Plus, they wanted him to take Dolly with him. "Hogan wanted Mike and me to leave Warner Pier," Dolly said. "They thought we should take cover in some secluded place. I won't mention just where because they might still use it."

She frowned. "I said I'd go, but later—while I was packing a bag—Mike hatched a new plan."

Dolly's face screwed up with distress. "He thought we should take Watt Wicker with us!"

"Watt? What on earth for? I mean, Hogan could find another hiding place for Watt."

Dolly shook her head. "It was some harebrained idea Mike had. I hadn't even realized Mike and Watt knew each other! Apparently they had been friends for years. Mike had never mentioned this to me before but he claimed they were pals, and he thought that he could get more information out of Watt than Hogan could."

I stared at Dolly for a few seconds. "Frankly, Dolly, that sounds silly. Hogan has a good reputation as an interrogator. He's well known in law enforcement circles for getting information out of people."

"I know. But most of those people were criminals. Mike thought that he and Watt might come up with some helpful information by collaborating. About midnight Mike called and dropped the idea on me!"

"So when Watt left the hospital in the middle of the night, he went with Mike?"

Dolly looked at me with eyes the size of bicycle tires. "You mean Mike actually took him?"

"I don't know. I guess Watt went off with *somebody.*" I just stared back at Dolly.

Dolly shook her head. "Honestly! I really love that guy, but sometimes I don't think he has the sense God gave a goose. Not that it's going to matter after our last conversation!"

"What do you mean?"

"Oh, Lee! Mike and I had a terrible fight! I told him I wouldn't go anywhere with them!"

"But that was the whole plan, Dolly."

"Not originally! At first Mike made it sound like this romantic rendezvous. Then I find out I'll be keeping house for him and Watt!"

"He and Hogan also wanted to keep you in a safe place."

"I felt safe until I heard Mike's plan." Dolly frowned. "Oh, I guess I acted childishly. But Mike had never before mentioned even *knowing* Watt Wicker, Lee. Now all of a sudden he wants the three of us to hide out together?" She looked up at me and glared. "Now I'm afraid I'll never see Mike again! And I'm not sure I want to!"

I didn't answer, purely because I didn't know what to say. Dolly didn't say anything either. But she sighed deeply, stood up, and walked into the kitchen, where I keep a box of tissues. Maybe she thought that blowing her nose would clear her brain.

Maybe the little pause cleared mine, because I thought of a simple question.

"Dolly, we're glad that you're here, glad you thought of us as a place where you can take refuge. But why? How did you pick this old farmhouse for a spot to light?"

Dolly looked at me and smiled. "You're the only people I know with a guest room!"

We both began to laugh. Then, before I could say anything more, I heard footsteps on the back porch. Joe's voice called out, "I'm home!"

Dolly grabbed my arm with both hands. "Does Joe have to know I'm here?"

"Yes," I said firmly. "This is his house, too. You can wait in the stairwell in case he has someone with him."

It was surprising how lightly Dolly could move as she ran for the stairwell. She flitted across the dining room and a corner of the living room and then disappeared behind the door that hid the steps to the second floor.

This had been one of Joe's days at the law firm, so he was wearing a suit. I greeted him at the door with a kiss.

"Nice day?" I asked.

He looked puzzled. "You look more cheerful than you did when I left this morning."

"I feel better. Dolly turned up."

"She turned up? Where is she? And where had she been?"

I took his hand and led him into the living room. I threw open the door to the stairwell and made a dramatic gesture.

"Ta-da!"

"Dolly!" Joe yelled a greeting, and the three of us went into a group hug, rocking back and forth and mumbling words like "Thank God" and "I'm so glad!" and "You scamp! Where did you go?" as we made very little effort not to rouse the entire neighborhood.

After a full minute of hugging, Joe let go but kept an arm around each of us. "There's only one bad thing about this reunion of pals," he said.

"What's that?" I asked.

"I have news. And it's not good news. Since we're all together, you two will have to hear it at the same time. The news is Watt Wicker has disappeared."

"We know Watt left the hospital. It's okay, Hogan thinks he's just wandered off."

"I'm afraid that idea has changed. Watt has really disappeared."

Dolly's voice got loud again. "But Mike agreed to keep him out of trouble!"

"Watt had mentioned Wildflower several times, and Mike thought the guy was headed out to her place, probably hitchhiking. Mike thought he would show up on her doorstep soon. But it's been—well, at least three or four hours, and Watt is not at Wildflower's. No one—not Wildflower, not Mike, not anybody else—seems to know where he is."

Chapter 14

"Honestly!" Dolly's voice shook. "That Mike! He was sure he could corral Watt."

"I'm sure he felt confident that he could do that. But I guess Watt was too sneaky for him. He's gone."

I jumped in then. "Joe, doesn't Mike have *any* idea where Watt has gone?"

"He says he doesn't." Joe made calming motions and urged both Dolly and me to sit down. Then he reported.

Joe told us Mike had taken Watt to a cottage Mike owned, located about two blocks from his own house. "It's still in Warner Pier," Joe said. "It was part of Mike's parents' estate. But it's sort of ramshackle and hidden by bushes and trees. Like a lot of things over there on the lakeshore."

Dolly was nodding vigorously, so I realized she must know about this cottage. "Mike works on that place when he gets time," she said. "It could be fixed up really cute. That's one reason he wanted the part-time job with the city and these other little jobs he's taken—to save up some extra money for that project. I think he'd really like to live in it."

Joe nodded. "Yeah, for a while Mike thought about selling it 'as is,' and he showed it to a few people. He took me over there because Hogan and I redid the Bailey house last year, and we talked about how much it would cost.

"The cottage needs a lot of work, but it would make a great place to live—or a cool rental. Mike probably thought that he and Watt could hide out there a few days, since only a few people know about it. So Hogan arranged for Mike to take Watt out of the hospital last night, and he and Watt spent the night there. Mike was keeping a close eye on Watt because of his head injury, and he told Hogan, who told me, that Watt was perfectly calm and seemed to rest okay. Then, this morning, Watt expressed a desire for a bowl of cereal."

Joe gestured again. "It seemed to be an innocent request. Mike had brought bacon and eggs along, but no cereal and no milk. So when Watt said he wanted to take a nap, Mike figured it was a good time to pick you up, Dolly. Plus, he could drive into Holland and buy milk and shredded wheat at the same time."

"Holland?" I was puzzled. "There are a dozen places to buy milk and cereal closer than Holland."

Joe nodded. "Mike says he was afraid to go to our very own Warner Pier Superette or closer places, because he was sure he'd run into someone he knew. Such as the checker. And Watt seemed calm and satisfied with staying at the cottage alone. But Watt may have been using his request as an excuse to get Mike out of the way. Because when Mike got back—after a little over an hour—no Watt. He had disappeared."

"And Mike has no clue where Watt has gone?"

Joe shook his head seriously. "Mike's wringing his hands,

mainly in frustration because Hogan wants him to stay under cover there at the cottage in case Watt comes back, and Mike wants to get out and scour the town looking for the guy. Of course, I guess Watt might have simply gone out for a long walk, but it's been quite a while now."

Joe went on talking. "There's one sighting. Katy and Darcy—I'm sure you remember them—claim that they saw him. But their story sounds sort of dumb."

"Where was he?"

"On the roof of the shoe shop. Sleeping."

That stopped the conversation for a few moments. We all stared at one another. And when someone spoke, it was Dolly.

"The roof of the shoe shop? How the heck would Katy and Darcy get up there?"

"Katy and Darcy weren't up there—they looked across the alley, and they swear they *saw* Watt."

Dolly frowned, and Joe went on. "The girls were moving out of their apartment. And the apartment has a clear view of the shoe shop's roof. When they saw Watt—or the guy they thought was Watt—apparently sleeping on that flat roof, they called Bill to tell him about it. But when they looked again, the person was gone."

"But why on earth would Watt be up on the roof?" Dolly asked. "And how would he get there?"

"Remember, there are built-in ladders at the back corners of that building—for fire safety or for repairmen. Getting there is easy. The question is, Why did Watt leave the cottage? And why would he climb to the roof of the store? Plus, was he really asleep?"

The three of us paused a moment to be puzzled.

"Well," Joe said, "we don't know the answer to those questions. But I do have one more piece of news. I talked to Mike, and I asked him to sneak out and come over here for dinner."

"Here?" I made a noise like a startled hostess. "I was going to give us canned tomato soup!"

"How about tomato pizza?" Joe asked.

Dolly nodded. "That should be fine. Mike won't expect a fancy meal. And I brought all the salad veggies I had, so they wouldn't spoil, in case I was gone several days. Do you have balsamic vinegar? And olive oil?"

Leave it to Dolly to come up with a gourmet salad dressing when all my refrigerator held was Kraft. By the time Mike's giant red truck pulled into our lane, she had torn up enough salad greens for four and shaken up a jar of something tart and tasty.

Neither Joe nor I asked Dolly if it was okay with her for Mike to join the party. If she and Mike wanted to continue their quarrel, they'd have to do it after dinner. We were more concerned with hiding his truck. Luckily it fit behind some bushes and trees next to our teensy garage. And at least it wasn't visible from the main road.

Dolly would never have gotten even her VW in our tiny garage if we hadn't already taken the picnic table and chairs out for the summer.

So Dolly made salad, Joe ordered pizza, and it turned into the easiest company dinner I ever served. The only things I contributed were red wine, Parmesan, and paper plates.

Conversation was easy, too. Dolly and Mike were so worried that they forgot they were mad at each other. Where was Watt? That was all we talked about. The words flowed until there was only one half of the second pizza left. That's when the phone rang.

Silence fell immediately. I know I was hoping it was someone with news about Watt.

"Okay," Joe said to Mike and Dolly, "you two are still hiding out, remember. Lee answers, and nobody else makes a sound."

I let the phone ring until I was sure everybody was with the program. Dolly even put her hand over her mouth.

Then the whole situation struck me as ridiculous. I laughed as I reached for the telephone. "It's probably somebody wanting to give me a lower interest rate on my credit card. Hello!"

"Lee?"

"This is she."

"It's Darcy. You know. Across the alley?"

"Of course. Darcy. I heard you and Katy were moving out today."

"Yes. I guess we're chicken. Katy and I decided we'd better give up the shoe business and try something else. But we wanted to thank you and Dolly for being so great to us last night."

"Oh, Darcy. We were so sorry that you two had to be mixed up in such a horrid event." Then I lied. "I've been thinking of the two of you all day. And Dolly and I are both hoping that things will go better for you in the future."

Actually I'd had so many other things on my mind that I'd barely thought of those two girls. Now I felt guilty. "Are you moving home?"

"Yes, we're each going to stay with our parents this summer. Next year we'll try getting out on our own again. Like I said, maybe we're chicken—"

"Oh, I don't think so!"

"We still don't know who was in the garage and scared us so bad. And the cops seem to think maybe nobody was in there. That we dreamed up the whole thing."

"I know you didn't."

"And when I think of poor Paige . . ."

"I know, Darcy. It's a tragic story."

"You know, Paige was so nice to us, but she couldn't seem to get her act together. She was always having man trouble."

I immediately thought of the conversation I had heard in Herrera's ladies' room. "Who had she been dating?"

"Some guy named Bob. Kinda old. I never learned his last name." Darcy gave a big sniff. "Anyway, if anybody needs us, Chief Jones has our phone numbers."

"If you get back to Warner Pier, be sure you drop by to see us."

"We will. Actually, we have to drop by the shoe store tomorrow to pick up our final checks. And this afternoon we went by TenHuis for one last bonbon, and we told Barbara and Dale good-bye."

"If I see you all looking in the display window, I'll stick out my tongue."

That made Darcy chuckle, and we hung up on a happier note.

I opened my mouth to ask Mike about who "his" Bob was, but Joe started talking before I could.

"Mike," he said, "just how well do you know Watt?"

"I've known him off and on a long time."

"How'd you meet him?"

"We worked together."

"What would you say are Watt's weaknesses?"

Mike nodded and looked out the window. "I see where you're going, Joe. Yes, way back when I first knew Watt, he used to put back a lot of booze. But I feel certain he's been dry for—oh, at least ten years now. If I wasn't confident of that, I'd have warned Lee, or anyone he worked for."

We dropped that subject, but I'm sure everyone put it in a mental pocket. Would we find Watt at the corner bar?

Everyone mulled that over for a moment, until I finally asked the question that had been puzzling me. "Mike, who is Bob?"

Chapter 15

My question was answered with complete silence. Mike simply stared at me. Then he gulped.

Finally he said, "There's a bunch of guys named Bob. It's a pretty common name."

"I mean the one you threatened a couple of weeks ago," I said.

Dolly gave a little gasp and stared at Mike.

"Did I threaten anyone?" Mike's eyes got squinty, and he looked at me sideways. "I don't remember doing that."

"This happened in the Warner Pier Rest-Stop, during the coffee club. Your phone rang, and you left the table to answer it. But all of us could still hear you."

Mike ducked his head over his pizza. "I couldn't have been serious, Lee." He took a big bite of salad.

"I don't think you were serious, Mike. But it sounded as if you were talking to somebody who owed you money."

Mike swallowed. "I guess he paid up. Because I've forgotten the whole episode."

"It was pretty dramatic," I said. "You said, 'I'll be over to see you . . . and I'm *not* bringing a lawyer.'"

Joe cleared his throat, then jumped into the conversation. "Mike, I always wonder where you come up with some of the colorful things you say."

"Everybody in my family talks a little crazy, Joe. I just repeat the things I grew up with."

"I guess we all do that," Joe said. "I had an uncle who used to mix up old sayings. He'd say, 'I'll do that even if it harelips the dog,' instead of the usual 'harelips the queen,' for example. And, Lee, I always wondered where you got that phrase you use sometimes: 'Each to his own taste, as the old maid said when she kissed the cow.'"

"My Texas grandmother used to say it, Joe. She said she got it from *her* grandmother."

The subject was successfully changed. Joe had flipped the topic of conversation, subtly taking Mike off the hot seat.

But I still did not know who Bob was. Mike had not answered my question. And I was not buying his claim that he didn't remember talking to Bob. In the Warner Pier Rest-Stop, in front of the whole coffee club.

But I shut up. For the moment. Apparently this was what Joe wanted me to do, and I trusted his judgment.

I'd ask why later.

I was still worried about Watt, of course. Then our not-very-happy gathering was interrupted by a knock at the front door.

Immediately, the four of us went into lockdown. Mike and Dolly tiptoed for the stairwell at quick march. Joe headed for the door, and I grabbed two place settings off the table, trying to make it look as if only two people had been eating.

I was throwing the paper plates away when I heard Joe. "Alex! Nice to see you. What brings you over?"

"I had an unexpected meeting, Joe."

I heard footsteps, and I looked out into the living room. Alex Gold was moving inside from the front porch. "I ran into someone I think you know." He gestured behind himself. I almost expected to hear him give a loud "Ta-da!"

And Watt stepped into the house.

Talk about excitement. "Watt!" Joe yelled. Dolly and Mike rushed in from their hiding place. I shouted. There was yelling, cheering, dancing, jumping—if our ceiling wasn't too low, I'd swear somebody did a cartwheel. I think I contributed a high kick and maybe shook a few imaginary pom-poms. Watt was hugged and kissed and escorted to the table, where he was offered pizza, iced tea, hot tea, coffee, ice cream, and, of course, bonbons. Dolly burst into tears. That made me cry.

It took several minutes before Joe whistled. "Quiet!" he yelled. "Does Hogan know he's here?"

"Well, no," Watt said.

Joe grabbed the phone and called Hogan while Dolly and I asked if Watt and Alex had eaten. Thank goodness we hadn't finished off the pizza.

Then the sirens began to sound. Three patrol cars showed up. Hogan jumped out of the first one and ran into the house. He pounded Watt on the back.

Watt smiled, but his eyelids drooped and he didn't have anything to say. He sat quietly, so quietly I wondered if he was fully conscious.

Gradually, everything calmed down. Hogan ran off the extra patrolmen, Watt and Alex were given food and drink—always Dolly's first priority—and Hogan asked the key question.

"Watt, where have you been?"

Watt looked at him without expression. "Chief, I was downtown, and I met Mr. Gold. But I don't know how I got there."

Hogan patted his shoulder. "I believe you need to be checked out by a doctor."

Watt looked at him narrowly. "Maybe so," he said. "Maybe so. I sure seem to have lost a day."

That put a damper on our excitement.

Mike was crushed and sure he had taken proper care of Watt. He kept saying, "But he seemed to be doing fine." Hogan kept saying this was merely a precaution, and Dolly announced that a bowl of chicken soup would probably fix Watt right up. I tried to keep my mouth shut, though I remember telling Joe, "He just seems to be confounded—I mean, confused!"

Hogan called an ambulance to take Watt back to the hospital for observation. But Watt told him he didn't really need to go.

"I'd talk if I knew anything about today," he said.

"Mike says he picked you up at the hospital yesterday evening," Hogan said. "Do you remember that?"

"Oh, sure. We went to a cottage he owns out on the lakeshore. Around Pilot's Point."

"What time did you get there?"

"About nine. I went to bed pretty soon after."

Mike nodded, agreeing with Watt's account. Watt continued. "I still felt pretty rocky. Bad headache. But I slept okay. I had a prescription. I got up around seven this morning."

"And?" Hogan was as deadpan as Watt.

"And nothing. Mike made eggs."

"You didn't eat them," Mike said.

"Those eggs were fine, Mike. I'm just not much of an egg eater."

Hogan nodded. "So you told Mike you'd rather have cereal."

"Well, yeah, Hogan. We all have our favorite foods, I guess. I felt pretty crummy, because of my head. And I like shredded wheat for breakfast."

"So you really wanted shredded wheat, and there wasn't any. Mike went to get you some cereal and milk. He also planned to pick up Dolly. He says you promised to stay at his house while he was gone."

Watt frowned deeply. "That's the part I don't remember, Chief. After he left, I had a cup of tea and then went back to bed. Just laid down in my clothes. Then I did go someplace, but I don't know how. It's like I was kidnapped."

Hogan didn't react to that. "Do you remember *where* you went?"

Watt thought hard. "Up on the roof . . . someone's roof somewhere."

"Why?"

"Well . . . could I have been lookin' for my truck, Chief?"

"Do you remember I told you we moved it to your house after you were injured?"

"I remember that *now*. Oh! And I remembered then, too, after a while. I started walking along one of those eastbound streets. But it's a long way from Mike's cottage to my house, out in the woods. So I started thumbin' a ride every time a car came along. Course, nobody stopped for me. So I finally stopped and leaned against a building." He shook his head gently, holding it as if it might fall off if he let go. Then his face brightened. "And somebody stopped to pick me up." His face lit up. "It was that Mr. Gold. The one who brought me here."

And that's where the story ended. Alex Gold said he had been climbing into his car when he saw Watt standing on the street, looking confused. Alex knew Watt because he had dickered with him about catching the raccoon in his shop's attic.

The Warner Pier PD was closed after five o'clock, and Alex didn't want to call 9-1-1 about Watt. So he put Watt into his car and brought him to our house simply because he knew we were friendly with him.

The ambulance came, and we all assured Watt that he was going to be okay. As the EMTs took Watt's vital signs, Joe tried to ask a couple of questions. "Watt, how did you get on the roof at Van's Shoes?" But Watt looked at him blankly and didn't answer.

"Watt!" Joe said. "Did you climb up on the roof? Or did someone, well, put you up there?"

Watt clutched at Joe's hand. "Mike?" he said. "Where's Mike?"

I looked around, and for the first time I realized that Mike and Dolly had disappeared. I spoke quietly to Joe. "Where did they go?"

Joe murmured in my ear. "Hogan sent them back into hiding."

The EMTs were closing up the ambulance when Bill Vanderwerp came running down the lane toward our little group.

"Hogan!" Bill seemed quite upset, waving for the ambulance to wait. "I'm not pressing charges against Watt! You can't arrest him!"

"Charge him with what?" Hogan asked.

This question seemed to confuse Bill completely. He muttered something about his roof, but when Hogan replied with more questions, Bill turned away, frowning.

Hogan assured Bill that Watt wasn't under arrest, simply headed to the hospital to check on his memory lapse. This seemed to cause Bill more confusion. He didn't look convinced about the wisdom of that action. He continued, speaking somewhat frantically. "Listen! Watt didn't do one thing to harm anything at the store. He didn't even eat anything. I don't want to press charges!"

Hogan assured Bill that he understood and that the hospital was for Watt's benefit.

"If you don't want to sign a complaint, Bill, this should be a short stay. But Watt's memory seems to be all messed up. The doctors need to figure out what's wrong. Then Watt will be released."

Bill still looked worried. "I feel terrible about this," he said. "I can't believe that Watt is the break-in artist who's been causing all this nuttiness."

His remark left me feeling astonished. "Bill!" I said. "I've heard some crazy gossip around this town, but that one takes the cake. Do you mean somebody suspected Watt of being one of the Cookie Monsters?"

Bill had the grace to look ashamed. "Well . . . well, I guess people were just trying to figure out who was new in town."

"Honestly!" I said. "On Tuesday they think Watt was attacked by the Cookie Monsters, and on Wednesday they think he's one of them!"

Joe whispered in my ear, "I could kiss you."

I whispered back, "Later, guy. But what brought that on?"

"The way you stick up for your friends always turns me on."

I was still fuming when Bill slunk away. But I was partly fuming at myself. What if Bill was right? What did I know about Watt? What did anybody know about Watt? He was a stranger to Warner Pier. What if those of us who liked him—Mike, Joe, Mike Herrera, Lindy, and even T. J.—were wrong?

Watt began waving his arms vigorously and making crazy beckoning motions—in my direction. One of the EMTs was about to close the ambulance's door, but I jumped over to the opening and stood there, blocking him.

"Hey, Watt!" I said. "Did you want to tell me something?"

"Lee, I don't know how long they're going to keep me. Could you and Mrs. Nettie go to my house and clean out the refrigerator? Please?"

Then he clutched my hand and spoke softly. "And make sure the trash is out."

Chapter 16

Naturally, I agreed. What I didn't say was "Great! That gives me a chance to prowl around in your stuff, Watt. Maybe I can figure out more about who you really are."

And maybe that was because Watt forestalled any idea I had about discovering his deep, dark secrets by saying, "There's not much stuff out there. I travel light."

Then he pressed a finger to his lips and closed his eyes. And what the heck did that mean?

Watt told us that Hogan had his keys. I assured him that Aunt Nettie and I would get rid of any food likely to spoil, and we'd freeze things we thought could be saved. I offered to bring in his mail, but Watt said he had a post office box.

As soon as the ambulance pulled out, Hogan gave me the house keys and told me how to find the house Watt was renting. It was near where Wildflower Hill lived, deep in the woods.

I hate to admit it, but I'm scared of the woods. My attitude about trees is a joke to my Michigan friends and relatives; they all know that masses of trees scare the bejabbers out of me.

I guess this mental tic developed from growing up on the

plains. North Texas is largely open country. Rural people there can see who's coming from all directions. So I'm wary if trees or hills block my view. I don't like it.

Our part of Michigan is as flat as Texas ever thought of being. But it's also covered with trees. I love my adopted home, but those trees—when I see them, here come the palpitations. My insides start to quiver.

Aunt Nettie and I decided to visit Watt's house before going to the shop the next morning. She said we should take one precaution; she called Wildflower Hill that night to tell her we were coming out. She said that Wildflower is information central for that neighborhood, and this might keep the neighbors from asking a lot of questions.

"Somebody might see your van and come over with a shotgun, just to make sure we weren't up to anything naughty," Aunt Nettie said. "But Wildflower will spread the word that we're coming and why."

After we decided that, we discovered that Mike and Dolly had really disappeared. But none of us worried, because Dolly left a note. "Thanks for the hospitality," it read. "I'll call you tomorrow."

This time I decided not to worry.

So the next morning Aunt Nettie and I followed a complicated set of turns and directions Hogan had given us. These led us to Watt's house, where we arrived around eight o'clock. Watt lived off the main route, on an unpaved road, surrounded by lots of trees.

"This has to be the place," I said, pointing to a black pickup. "At least that's Watt's truck in the yard."

"And that's his raccoon trap in its bed," Aunt Nettie said.

"Hogan said he had asked Jerry to load it up when Watt went into the hospital the first time." She pulled the key out of her purse, and I parked my van next to the truck.

The house was small, very small, and was standard woodland style. The siding had been stained brown, but was now faded to a reddish color, and the house had a low roof. Behind the cabin was the butane tank and a small storage shed. Stretching across the front was a simple porch with two steps up and a door smack in the middle. On the porch were two lawn chairs, the kind made of aluminum frames with faded cloth seats and backs.

The house was what the early settlers would have built if they'd had access to a lumber mill, instead of relying on logs as building material.

The key opened the front door easily, and Aunt Nettie and I stepped inside. The house had only one room, and to our surprise, there was a light on over the sink.

We looked at each other. Then I yelled a greeting. "Hello! Anybody here?"

There was no answer, but we still looked around. No one was in the tiny bathroom or the small closet. I even checked under the bed. No one there. I looked out the back door. The tiny porch was empty except for a broom and a mop propped against the wall.

"I guess the last person in here left the light on," I said.

"There aren't many places to hide," Aunt Nettie said. "I think we've checked all of them, and there's no one here. I'll tackle the refrigerator."

"I'll dump the trash and check the cupboards."

It was easy work. Aunt Nettie poured spoiled milk down

the sink and stuffed brown lettuce into a large plastic trash bag she had brought along. The meat in the small freezer compartment—a package of hamburger and a small plastic sack holding two pork chops—was still frozen, so we left it, along with the ketchup, mustard, and mayonnaise. I left the crackers and cereal in their boxes and the sugar in a plastic container with a sealable lid. Two little wastebaskets were emptied into Aunt Nettie's big trash bag. A small pile of laundry went into a separate bag. Aunt Nettie said she would wash it.

The furniture had obviously come with the little house. A sleeping bag covered a double bed with a stained mattress. Near a small table was a worn couch. A cheap floor lamp, two chairs, a small TV set, and some checked curtains just about finished the decor. A TV tray stood at one end of the couch. On it were a pencil and paper, with the daily sudoku half-worked. At the other end of the couch was a small chest of drawers. Its three drawers held nothing but underwear and socks. Shirts and pants hung in the closet. None of it looked significant.

The most distinctive decoration was a giant mounted fish hanging over the couch; and on the wall above the bed was a set of eight-by-ten action photos of fishermen. The photos were terrific!

I told Aunt Nettie about Watt's request for me to check over the trash, so she and I both looked through the contents of the wastebaskets. Neither of us saw anything worth saving; just mass-market begging letters and special offers for cell phones.

We couldn't find a garbage can, only the two small wastebaskets. When I pointed this out, Aunt Nettie didn't act too surprised. "Watt probably takes his garbage to the dump in bags," she said.

"But wouldn't he need someplace to store the garbage until he takes it?"

We both shrugged that problem off. Then Aunt Nettie spoke. "The most surprising thing is how clean this place is."

I agreed. "Yes, I can see why Mike hired Watt to clean kitchens. He's a neat and clean guy. And he told me he traveled light."

"It's a sad way to live," Aunt Nettie said. "Everything Watt owns fits in his truck."

"Or maybe it's a smart way. I sure collect too much stuff. I don't know who's smarter—Watt or me!"

I went to the window over the sink and peered out, taking another look at the area behind the cabin.

"Huh," I said. "There's a building out back."

I moved aside so Aunt Nettie could see. "It seems to be just a shed," she said. "I can't tell for sure. It's a light color."

We opened a back door and stepped out onto a minuscule porch. About thirty feet away, at the end of a path, was a small metal shed. A clothesline stretched from the back door to the shed, and two dish towels hung on it. Aunt Nettie took the towels down.

"I wonder what's in there," I said. "Knowing Watt, probably pet skunks."

Aunt Nettie chuckled. "Oh, Lee! I can't imagine that. I suppose Watt might have kept the raccoons he caught there, but I'm sure he wouldn't have forgotten to mention an animal who needed feeding."

Aunt Nettie walked over to the shed and tried to loosen its latch, but the door didn't open. She reached into her pocket, but the first of Watt's two keys wouldn't open the door.

"This lock is jammed," Aunt Nettie said. After a quick rattle of the door, she pulled the key out of the lock and began to examine it.

Then I heard the faintest possible noise inside the shed. What could that be?

I took a split second to listen to the door; as I listened, I watched. And the door moved, just a bit. Not the handle—that didn't move. But the door itself moved, ever so slightly. As if somebody were leaning against it.

A shiver went down my back. Could someone—something—be behind that door?

All I knew was that Aunt Nettie was with me. She was a plump woman in her sixties, and she couldn't run if a monster jumped out at us.

And she was pulling out another key and getting ready to put it into the keyhole.

Suddenly I was positive that if we opened the door, some ghastly thing would erupt out of that shed.

I clutched Aunt Nettie's arm. "I told Watt I wouldn't poke through his stuff. Let's leave this and head for the office. I'm sure there's nothing perishable in that little shed."

Aunt Nettie looked surprised. Then she shrugged. "Probably not," she said. "We can ask Watt later."

She put the keys back in her pocket. We turned around and slowly walked to the back door. I tried to hustle Aunt Nettie along, but she strolled slowly. That's the way she walks on an outdoor path.

Once inside the house, I grabbed up my trash sacks. "I'll take Watt's sudoku to him, and let's scram. The trees are getting me down."

Aunt Nettie laughed. Before we left, we turned out all the lights, including the one over the sink. Then we turned the porch light on, even though it was daylight. I threw the garbage bags and laundry into the backseat of the van and locked the door. Then we climbed in, and we beat it. I drove a steady pace for the mile back to the county road. I couldn't speed on that rough gravel road, even though my instincts were chanting, "Run-run-run-hurry-hurry-hurry."

As I drove, I asked Aunt Nettie to pull my phone out of my purse and call the police station. She got Hogan and told him about our visit to Watt's. While she was chatting, I kept repeating, "Let me talk to him. Let me talk to him." This mystified her, and several times she replied, "In a minute, Lee."

She didn't understand what had suddenly upset me, but she finally said, "Hogan, dear, Lee wants to talk to you. I'm not really sure what it's about."

I grabbed the phone from her. "Hogan! I could swear there was somebody at Watt's house! Watching us!"

Chapter 17

Aunt Nettie's mouth fell open, and Hogan's voice got hard. "Did anybody threaten you? Hurt you? Chase you?"

Of course, I had to reply "no" to all of his questions.

Then I told him about spooky feelings and a movement in the shed.

"Hogan! I admit I didn't see a soul! Didn't hear a sound! Am I losing it? Has my mind finally just gone? But I saw that door move—just slightly—and if Aunt Nettie hadn't been with me, I swear I would have turned and run! I thought I'd never get Aunt Nettie into the van!"

There was a long silence before Hogan spoke. "You're usually pretty calm, Lee. Jerry and I will go on out there and take a look at the situation."

I breathed a sigh of relief. "You'll need Watt's keys. Can we wait for you at the Rest-Stop?"

"Good enough."

As soon as I hung up, I glanced at Aunt Nettie. She looked concerned, but not panicky.

"I'm sorry," I said. "Maybe I'm losing my mind."

She smiled and patted my arm. "We'd better invent a signal. When you need to tell me it's time to panic, you'll have to say something or do something so I get the idea."

I tried to laugh. "Like run up a red flag?"

"Too obvious, Lee. Maybe something like patting your head and rubbing your stomach."

That made me laugh for real. "Aw, c'mon, Aunt Nettie! You know how uncontaminated—I mean, uncoordinated! You know how uncoordinated I am. I'd be sure to pat my stomach and rub my head and get you all confused."

Pulling into the Warner Pier Rest-Stop was quite a relief. It's on the eastern edge of Warner Pier, so we were almost out of those thick, scary woods. Plus, we hadn't seen a soul on the road for the whole trip.

"We made it," I said. "And no one followed us."

Aunt Nettie smiled. "I thought there was some kind of truck way back behind us for a few minutes. But it disappeared. Now that we're here, do you want to get a cup of coffee while we wait for Hogan?"

"Not until we've handed Watt's keys over. I'm sure Hogan is on his way here."

We watched the cars in the parking lot for a moment. Joe was working at his office in Holland that day, so his truck wasn't there. However, a few of the coffee club members' trucks were parked in the lot. One truck had Digger Brown's plumbing company logo, and another bore the address and phone number of Tony Herrera's machine shop on the door. The doughnut delivery van driven by R. L. Lake pulled in at the side of the station. He was running a little late that morning. He waved at us, then took out a big box of doughnuts and went inside.

It was comforting to see the familiar sights of morning at the Rest-Stop.

Then Hogan's chief of police car pulled in and threw a little gravel as he made a quick stop beside my van. He walked over to us, opened the passenger's door, gallantly gave Aunt Nettie a kiss on the cheek, and then moved her to the backseat of the van.

When I offered him Watt's keys, he shook his head. "Mike had a set Jerry was able to pick up," he said.

He sat in the passenger's seat and interrogated me. This process caught me by surprise. I was beginning to feel pretty silly about my fear out at Watt's house. Maybe I had imagined the whole thing.

But Hogan seemed to take my feelings seriously. He had me go over our visit to the cabin step-by-step, and I described its neatness, its loneliness, its silence. But now that I was out of the woods—yuk, yuk—there was very little that had specifically been threatening.

"See, Hogan," I said, "everything in the atmosphere out there combined to feel soupy—I mean, spooky! But nothing happened. I've acted like an idiot and dragged you out here over nothing."

Hogan ignored that and asked me another question. "Tell me again about how the shed's door moved."

"Just barely! It only moved slightly. Maybe it was my imagination. Or if it did move, maybe the motion was caused by something else. The wind, maybe. Or, you know, just the fact that Aunt Nettie and I were touching the shed might have made it wiggle."

Aunt Nettie leaned forward. "But we weren't touching it, Lee. I had taken a step back to examine the keys, and you never touched the shed. You stood behind me, and you would have had to reach around me to put your hand on any part of the shed. I would have noticed. I'm sure you never touched the building."

Hogan frowned, staring into space. "I'm sorry I let you two go out there alone."

His remark surprised me. "Why? Last night neither you nor Joe had any problem with our going out there to do Watt a favor. Why should you expect something to frighten us?"

There was a long pause before Hogan answered. "After the doctor examined Watt this morning, he called me. It seems most peculiar, but he thinks one of the likeliest reasons for Watt's mental fog is that he was drugged."

Drugged? I couldn't take in the meaning of the word. "What are you saying, Hogan?"

"I'm saying that either Watt used some sort of drug voluntarily, or—"

"No! Oh, golly, Hogan!" I said. "I can't believe that. Or maybe I don't want to believe it."

Hogan kept on talking. "Or maybe someone drugged his food or drink, Lee. And Mike says in all the time he's known Watt, he's never known him to use drugs. Except alcohol. I think he may have had a problem with that at one time. And apparently Mike and Watt have known each other a lot longer than they've been admitting."

I clutched the steering wheel and clamped my mouth shut. I wanted to explain to Hogan that his idea about Watt taking drugs deliberately was totally wrong. But, heck—I didn't know Watt all that well.

My head was spinning. What was happening? Did Hogan know anything else? If he did, would he tell me? I had to ask.

"Was Mike affected?" I asked. "Was he drugged?"

"No. But all that means is that Watt ate or drank something that Mike didn't."

"Does this make Mike a suspect?"

"Not to anybody who knows him. Out of context, it might make Mike look guilty, but he's smarter than that. What Mike *is* guilty of," Hogan said, "is not taking the whole situation seriously. He took Watt out to the lonely cottage last night, supposedly to keep him safe. But he barely remembered to lock the door. When I went out there this morning, for example, he had left all the windows open, 'for air.' Anybody could have gotten in. Anybody could have put drugs in any of the food or drink in the place. And maybe somebody did."

The three of us sat silently for a minute. Then Hogan's two-way radio crackled. Hogan answered. "Jerry?"

We could all hear Jerry Cherry's reply. "Hogan, did Lee and Nettie say Watt's place was ultra-neat?"

"Yah. They were both quite impressed."

"They might not be impressed now. It looks to me as if somebody tossed it."

Aunt Nettie gasped, and I yelled, "Oh no!"

Hogan jumped out of my van and into his own car. All of us took off east again, headed for the deep woods.

Looking back, I have no idea why Aunt Nettie and I followed Hogan. We were not law officers. If something had happened to Watt's house, she and I were not going to be any help. But Hogan could have called my cell phone and told us to stay put, even while we were driving, and he didn't. So we tore down the gravel road, headed for the tiny cabin in the woods.

After we got there, naturally, Hogan and Jerry wouldn't

even let us pull onto the property. We sat on the county road while three carloads of police—city, county, and state—arrived to look over a building about large enough to hold three of Santa's elves.

But no one told us to go home, so we waited, watching the important law enforcement business going on. It felt like hours. I sighed deeply and looked at my watch; we'd been there all of twenty minutes. When I reported this to Aunt Nettie, we both laughed.

Shortly after that, the Michigan State Police mobile lab showed up, and we got a better idea of why nothing was going on. They'd been waiting for the lab guys to show, indicating that Hogan thought there might be evidence to be found in the little house.

About ten minutes after the lab techs showed up, Hogan came to collect Aunt Nettie and me. We put protective booties over our shoes and were escorted to the cabin. I probably strutted toward it; I felt quite important to be part of an investigation.

Until Hogan spoke. "Don't touch anything," he said sternly. "Not a single thing."

Aunt Nettie and I nodded meekly.

"All we want is for the two of you to confirm that the room doesn't look like it did when you left."

We nodded. Then he opened the door.

Aunt Nettie stepped inside. She gasped loudly. I stepped in. I yelped. "This place looks like a tornado hit!"

Gone was the neat little room with clean dishes stacked on open shelves, silverware in orderly rows on a tray, a tidy bed with a sleeping bag cover. In its place were stacks of papers thrown any which way, dishes smashed everywhere, bedding tossed on the floor, and silverware scrambled into heaps.

I was mystified. "Were they searching for something?"

Aunt Nettie was wringing her hands, and I put my arm around her shoulders. "Oh, Lee," she said. "It looks like a devil got loose in here. Were the intruders just angry?" Her voice was distressed.

"You're right. The room looks as if a child had a tantrum in here."

I tried to sound practical. "Well, let's look it over and see what's different. Maybe we can tell Hogan what's gone."

I got a notepad from my purse, and we began to look over the scene.

One of the first things we looked at was the mysterious shed, and we found it standing open and completely empty. I was disappointed.

"What a letdown!" I said. "I guess I really did imagine the whole shed scare."

But Hogan came up behind us and cleared his throat. After Aunt Nettie and I had jumped several feet high, he spoke. "It wasn't your imagination. Look at the floor."

The dirt floor was covered with footprints.

I gave a gasp that made Aunt Nettie grab my arm. "Lee," she said. "There *was* somebody there!"

I pointed out that the prints might have been there from an earlier visit by someone, but Hogan ignored me.

Hogan shooed the two of us back into the house. Aunt Nettie stopped just inside the door.

"Isn't it odd," Aunt Nettie said, "that the drawers haven't been dumped?"

"That's right. All of this mess came off the shelves. There aren't many cupboards or drawers, true, but the intruders seemed more interested in breaking things than in looking at them. Why would they toss things around like that?"

"Were they simply throwing things because they were mad?"

"I just realized one thing that isn't here," I said. "There was junk mail in the wastebaskets, which we emptied. But there's no 'real' mail either. No bills, no letters, no personal mail!"

Aunt Nettie nodded. "Of course, Watt said he had a postal box."

"Yes, and all this junk mail is addressed to it. Watt apparently brought that mail home and threw it out. Or threw out unwanted mail at the post office. But there should be mail he would keep. Letters from home, birthday cards, notices of a class reunion, credit card bills."

Aunt Nettie's voice was sad. "Doesn't Watt have any friends or relatives?"

German Chocolate Cake—Yum, Yum!

(The Chocolate Snowman Murders)

No recipe included here, but you can find it on the back of the German's Sweet Chocolate package. And I found this cake's history fascinating.

One of America's favorite desserts—Baker's German's Sweet Chocolate Cake—is neither "Baker's" nor "German."

Commonly known as German chocolate cake, this is a delicately flavored light chocolate cake made with a particular brand of sweetened cooking chocolate. Between each of its three layers and on top is a caramel icing packed with pecans and coconut.

Baker's Chocolate is not, as you might think, called that because it was formulated for the exclusive use of bakers; it was simply the utterly appropriate family name of the chocolate company's founder.

And Baker's popular product, German's Sweet Chocolate, was named after Samuel German, a Baker's employee who came up with the sweet cooking chocolate in 1852.

At that time most chocolate was still used for making beverages, but in 1870 Baker's published a twelve-page booklet of baking recipes. But we're not there yet—German chocolate cake was not in that booklet.

German chocolate cake was *apparently* invented almost ninety years later by a Texas woman who submitted the recipe to a Dallas newspaper in 1957. She named her creation German's Chocolate Cake after the chocolate she used to make it. The recipe swept the nation (and lost its apostrophe somewhere along the way, thus creating the widespread impression that German immigrants had brought the dessert to America).

And now, June 11th is National German Chocolate Cake Day!

Chapter 18

Hogan let us wander around for a few minutes, then he firmly led us back to my van. He assigned Jerry Cherry to escort us back to Warner Pier and sent us away.

"Don't talk about this lack of personal mail," he said. "I don't want Watt to hear about it before I can question him. He may have tossed it himself. Maybe he deliberately broke all contact with family and friends."

I guess his instructions were one reason we speculated about the mail all the way back to the office.

Aunt Nettie seemed really puzzled. "Why would the burglars make such a mess? And apparently not take anything else? Unless they took some papers. And they may not have. Maybe Watt simply hadn't collected his mail for a month!"

"Or maybe they did take something else. We didn't take an inventory."

"If we missed something, it wasn't anything very large."

Our speculations, of course, were more annoying than helpful to both of us. I think we were both pleased to get back to a parking spot in our alley so we couldn't talk about this incident anymore.

Jerry Cherry was still following us, and we both waved good-bye to him with pleasure. He had barely turned the corner when we heard a loud voice from farther up the alley. Looking around, we saw Alex Gold waving at us from the porch of his own shop.

"Hey, Lee and Nettie! Hang on a minute before you go inside. I have a special invitation for you both."

We stood on our porch, waiting while he walked quickly down the alley toward us. Alex was beaming happily. "Ladies, I'm having a party."

Aunt Nettie smiled. "Just what we need, Alex. Things have been pretty dismal lately."

"This is going to be a great party! And it is a party. I'm asking all the downtown merchants over for a champagne breakfast tomorrow at the new shop. And bring your husbands and wives, and your girlfriends and boyfriends, and your sweethearts and pals!"

"Is the shop ready to open?" Aunt Nettie asked. "I didn't think it was finished."

"It's not. This is a preopening event. Come and go. Eight to ten a.m. It's the secret kickoff of the real thing."

"But, Alex," I said, "what good is a 'secret' kickoff? A kickoff event is supposed to draw in customers. If nobody knows about it, it's a waste of time."

Alex beamed ever more broadly. "It's a preview of something that's going to knock Warner Pier onto its backside with excitement! I can hardly wait to see your reactions!"

He turned around, chortling. "You're going to be really impressed. Eight o'clock tomorrow morning. At the store. You're going to love it! And Herrera's is doing the food."

"Yum! Yum!" Aunt Nettie said. "We'll be there."

I shook my head as we watched him trot up the alley. "What do you suppose he's up to?"

"Some special jewelry that's too expensive for most ordinary tourists to buy," Aunt Nettie said. "I don't know Alex as well as you and Joe do, but he always seems excited about something."

"At least we get breakfast," I said.

Then we opened the back door to TenHuis Chocolade and found a madhouse. No real disasters, I suppose. But when two of three bosses—one of us chocolate and the other money—were three hours late to work, and the third boss, Dolly, wasn't coming in at all, the morning was destined for trouble.

It took a while, but we got it straightened out. Aunt Nettie got the chocolate schedule back on track, and I returned calls and took orders that the clients swore were desperate emergencies. By one o'clock we had all the serious challenges handled, and I told Aunt Nettie I was ready for lunch.

"Me, too," Aunt Nettie said. "Bunny is back from her lunch break. I suppose that the two of us could dash down to the corner for twenty minutes and get something to eat."

"Terrific idea," I said. "And while we're waiting for our sandwiches, maybe I'll call Wildflower Hill and see if she knows another raccoon trapper. I'm afraid Watt is simply not going to be able to get the job done. Not while Hogan is trying to keep him undercover. And Mike is unavailable."

About half the time, I hate my cell phone, because it always rings when it's in the bottom of my purse in the back bedroom.

The rest of the time, I can't live without it. The call to Wildflower fulfilled both situations.

First, she wanted to hear all about the excitement at Watt's house. And, of course, I wasn't supposed to tell her anything.

"Huh," I said. "How did you hear about it? Hogan told us to keep the whole innocent—I mean, incident! The whole incident under wraps. He threatened us with a good scolding if we told anybody anything."

"Hogan's smart enough to know that plan won't work in a neighborhood like mine."

I was having trouble picturing the deep, dark forest where Wildflower and Watt lived as a "neighborhood," so I apparently didn't answer her question as quickly as she expected. She prodded me for a reaction. "Well, Lee? What's going on?"

Could I tell her an abbreviated version and satisfy both Hogan and Wildflower? I had to try.

"Watt had to go back to the hospital," I said. "He asked Aunt Nettie and me to go out to his house and make sure there was nothing in his fridge that would spoil. When we got there, we felt—well, afraid. We were afraid that somebody had been prowling around. Things seemed disturbed. Since we'd never been to Watt's house before, we weren't sure. When we told Hogan about our fears, he sent somebody out there to double-check. And the person he sent could tell that there had definitely been an intruder."

"Did that really call for six patrol cars?"

"Six? Were there six?"

"That's the gossip. Three from Warner Pier—and we're outside the city limits—plus one from the county, and two state cops. Naturally, the neighbors all gathered around to stare, too. Plus, later on, the state cops went house-to-house asking if any of us had seen anything. I guess they talked to everybody."

"Did you? See anything?"

"What would I see?"

"Oh, a strange car, a strange person—you know, anything out of the ordinary. Strange."

She sighed. "You know, Lee, I know you don't like the deep woods, but our area isn't really that remote. We're not strange; we just like cheap places to live."

"I know, I know, you told me! You back up to the Fox Creek Nature Preserve. It has hiking trails. People walk by all the time."

My sarcasm didn't amuse Wildflower. "That's right. But nobody walked by this morning. Not that I saw. The only thing unusual—and it's not even that out of the ordinary—was the chopper."

"Chopper? As in helicopter?"

"Yes, the forestry service patrols an area near here." Then she spoke darkly. "Or that's what they claim. It comes by about once a week. Watt says he'd like a ride 'for old times' sake.'"

"Wildflower—"

Before I could finish my sentence, she took a sudden, deep breath. "Gotta go!"

"She hung up on me!" I said with a groan of annoyance.

"I see the waitress coming with our lunch," Aunt Nettie said. "Eat first, call back later."

"But I didn't get to ask her about a raccoon trapper."

"She'll probably just recommend Mike."

"I don't think Hogan would like that idea. He certainly doesn't want Mike fooling around in an area that seems remote anymore. Not until this situation is resolved."

I gave up on the idea of trapping our alley raccoon and ate my sandwich. The whole thing seemed rather pointless. But before we even finished our dessert—ice cream with a fancy cookie—Wildflower called back.

"I guess you're going to need another raccoon trapper," she said.

"How'd you know? I didn't even mention it."

"I'm clairvoyant. Also, with Watt in the hospital, it was pretty obvious."

She gave me the name and number of a man over near the county seat. Then she hung up again. I had the feeling I wasn't on Wildflower's list of all-time favorite people. But maybe she hadn't given up on me.

However, as it ended up, I didn't call the new raccoon trapper. Mike called me as soon as I was back at my desk. In fact, he called me so promptly that I suspected he had seen me arrive at the shop. Was he up in Dolly's apartment? He and Dolly should have been hiding out still.

Mike spoke so quickly that I didn't get the chance to ask where he was.

"Hey, Lee, I guess all this commotion is leaving you without a raccoon catcher."

"That seems to be the case. I sure don't want you or Watt wandering around in the dark alley where the boogeymen seem to be hanging out."

"I'm not too worried, but Hogan is. And Dolly. But surely we'll get it all straightened out pretty quick."

"I sure hope so. Though I'm much more worried about you and Watt than about the raccoons."

"Yeah. Watt—well, he almost needs a full-time keeper. Has for years."

"When did you first meet Watt?"

Mike hesitated. "Oh, long time back. He's a smart guy, but he can be kind of spacey."

A suspicion began to boil up in my mind. Could I ask? I took a deep breath and jumped right in.

"Mike? Did you know Watt in the army?"

Mike hesitated as long as I had before he answered. "How'd you get that idea?" he said. "Give the guy a chance. And if he wants to help Bob, let him."

The line went dead.

Chapter 19

"Give the guy a chance," Mike had said.

Why did Watt need a chance? Watt had mentioned a helicopter ride—"for old times' sake." Had Mike and Watt known each other in the army? Had they flown in the same helicopters? Did Hogan know if they had been in the army together? Did it matter? What was all this about, anyway? Should I try to find out? Or was I simply being nosy?

I stood at my desk for at least a minute, considering the possibilities. Then I shrugged my shoulders. I couldn't continue trying to figure out other people's motivations and intentions. I had to get on with my life.

So there, Mike.

I still quizzed Hogan about the whole ordeal when we talked on the phone late that afternoon. I detailed the exchange of questions and—sort of—answers with Mike.

Hogan replied, "Hmm."

"Is that it, Hogan? Your only comment?"

"Yep."

I thought a moment. "Okay. Your call. I guess it's sometimes better not to ask too many questions. But I will ask one more. Are Dolly and Mike in a safe place?"

"Yes. This time. I'm sorry I didn't handle that better last time."

"Your record is pretty good," I said. "I'll talk to you later."

Yes, Hogan now seemed to have everybody safe. Including Dolly.

In fact, where was Dolly?

I went into the workshop and looked around. No sign of her. Had she taken refuge with Mike?

Aunt Nettie was at her desk in the alcove off the kitchen, so I asked her.

She smiled. "Yes, she's with Mike. Hogan sent the two of them off."

"Are they with Watt?"

"That I don't know. But Hogan assures me that they are in a much more secure place than the first time. Mike—he's overconfident. He thinks he can handle anything."

"I guess a guy his size can handle most things."

I turned to go to my own office, but Aunt Nettie stopped me. "Dolly did tell me one strange thing. Maybe you and Joe could check it out."

"Sure. What was it?"

"She thinks she heard footsteps . . ." She leaned toward me and lowered her voice almost to a whisper. "Upstairs."

"Upstairs? Upstairs from her apartment? On the roof?"

Aunt Nettie shrugged. "It sounds crazy."

"It certainly does. There's no way to get there except through her apartment or on those ladders on the back of the building."

"I guess I could ask Hogan to look up there."

"Oh heck! I can go. There's not going to be anything but hot asphalt."

"Be careful, Lee."

Nearly all the buildings in the business district of Warner Pier have flat roofs. The area was built between 1890 and 1910, and that's the way small-town commercial structures were designed in that era.

The buildings in our small downtown are brick with white trim, or they're white frame. No mid-century modern or even Prairie School for our merchants. The design of homes in Warner Pier varies greatly, but not the design of our businesses.

The two buildings Aunt Nettie and I combined to create a home for TenHuis Chocolade are typical of the era. In the early days of the twentieth century, red brick was the rule for small-town businesses, and we hold up the fashion loyally.

Though TenHuis expanded to fill three floors of two buildings, including full use of our two basements, we definitely fit in with the local tradition.

And our second floors fit the standard style, too. Both buildings had small apartments upstairs. Historically the proprietors lived in them; today, both of ours have been rented out.

The roofs are almost flat, with short parapets on all four sides. An architect told me that the roofs were originally weatherproofed with "coal tar pitch." Over the years, the roofing material had changed to be some sort of plastic sheets laid over insulation, and air-conditioning units had been placed atop the buildings. Walkways crisscrossed the roofs here and there for access to mechanical equipment while protecting the roofing from wear.

I wasn't scared to go up there. The only danger was if I stepped over the edge of the parapet and fell two stories to the sidewalk. Reasonable caution would avoid that.

I unlocked the desk drawer in which I kept spare keys, and took out the duplicates to Dolly's apartment. I was surprised that she and Mike hadn't checked on the sound Dolly heard coming from the roof before they left. They probably didn't have time.

It took me only a few minutes to go out the back door of the shop and up the stairway leading to Dolly's apartment. Once there, I unlocked her door, using my landlord keys, and glanced around. Dolly had, as usual, left everything ultra-neat.

I then unlocked the door that led to the roof. When the door opened, I saw the narrow stairway, almost steep enough to be called a ladder. A single lightbulb hung from the stairwell's ceiling, giving dim illumination. There was a handrail, and I clung to it as I went on up. At the top, another door with a sturdy lock led to the roof.

When I opened it, the late-afternoon sunlight was blinding, and I shaded my eyes with my hand. I stepped over the sill and stood still until my eyes adjusted to the powerful light.

After a moment, I saw that the trees the city fathers had planted along the sidewalks stood higher than the roof, so while most of the roof was roasted by the sun, there were some small areas of shade.

I began a solemn procession around the building, scanning for anything unusual. I first went along the front wall, taking a long look across the street at my mother-in-law's insurance office building. It always looked classy and businesslike. Even though she and her husband, Joe's stepfather, were in Seattle for a convention of insurance professionals, the office still appeared to be open and operating according to her rules.

Joe's mom, Mercy, runs most of her life with an iron hand. But Joe had always gone his own way. As a single mom, how did she resist micromanaging her only son? Or was it that Joe resisted being managed? I certainly have never managed him, but he was never unmanageable.

I looked up and down the street, enjoying my unusual vantage point. Tourists, dogs, kids, and more tourists. It was too early in the season for the shops to be packed, but there were plenty of people walking by.

I turned left and walked to the roof of our second building. The architect and the builder had made our double structure look like a single building, just as we asked. The second-floor windows flowed smoothly from building to building. I could see both buildings reflected in Mercy's big front windows; it looked pretty good.

At the corner of the building, I turned left again and walked back seventy-five feet, reaching the alley. I could see the cars parked behind the stores and the Dumpster where Hogan's searchers had found the packing pads. I still didn't understand those. Turning around, I had an expansive view of Alex Gold's roof. It was just as smooth and lacking in detail as ours was, although our air-conditioning equipment loomed in the back corner of the roof. I carefully circled it.

And I almost broke a leg on a stick.

It was jutting out from under the AC unit. I caught my toe on it, tripped, and nearly went sprawling flat on my face.

Luckily, I was able to catch myself on the corner of the AC

equipment. Plus, I had on long khaki slacks, so when I fell to my knees, I didn't skin them.

I broke my silence, however, letting go with a few stout words suitable for the occasion, such as "Oh dear!"

I knelt there until I caught my breath. Then I pulled the stick out and examined it. "What on earth?"

It wasn't a stick from a tree. It was actually a heavy metal rod with smaller pieces of metal and lots of tiny hinges attached to it. Black rags festooned the smaller pieces of metal. It even had a crooked handle. I knew what it was almost immediately.

"Good heavens!" I said. "It's an umbrella!"

Then I laughed.

I got to my feet and stood there examining the umbrella. It must have blown there, I decided.

I pictured the wrecked umbrella rolling around the rooftop in even a light wind, or tossed back and forth in torrents of rain.

No wonder Dolly had thought she heard footsteps. The umbrella would definitely have made noises as it traversed the asphalt and gravel—thunking and bumping around. But why hadn't it blown off the roof?

I tucked the umbrella under my arm and completed my trek around the roof. I found nothing else unusual, so I relocked all the doors and went downstairs.

I walked into Aunt Nettie's office, brandishing the shattered umbrella over my head.

"Hey," I called out. "Mary Poppins has been on our roof!"

Aunt Nettie laughed. Bunny laughed. Everybody laughed. We all marveled at how on earth a tattered and worn umbrella wound up on our roof.

"That's a hoot!" "What are the odds?" "It really must have been Mary Poppins!"

I hung the umbrella on the hall tree in the corner of Aunt Nettie's office. She found a box of tough rubber bands and used a half dozen to keep the umbrella's ribs from flopping around.

"I'll show this to Hogan," she said, "and tell him where you found it. He'll think that's hilarious."

"I'm going home," I said. "I don't really care how this bumbershoot came to land on top of our building."

"Neither do I," Aunt Nettie said. "By the way, I had the ladies make up a tray of chocolate critters as a gift for Alex."

I peeked to see what she'd tucked inside the box. Beavers of dark chocolate, squirrels and raccoons of milk chocolate, bunnies of white chocolate.

"Fantastic! He'll be pleased. If he and Garnet don't want them for the breakfast, they'll do for later."

"I thought I'd try to get there early tomorrow," she said. "Then I can come on to the shop without being too late."

I sighed. "I hope it doesn't drag on too long. Alex makes things such a big deal. I'd just as soon start the day with something low-key."

"Not likely for him," Aunt Nettie said.

Little did we know that low-key was the last thing the day would bring.

Chapter 20

The next morning Joe and I showed up at Gold's Jewelry at eight thirty a.m. for Alex's preopening breakfast for his fellow merchants.

The streets were not exactly bumper-to-bumper that early—this was Warner Pier, after all, and there aren't a huge number of merchants in the town. But as we drove down Peach Street, we could see that plenty of people were going through the front door of the new shop.

"I guess Alex's plan to get attention is working," I said.

"I think he's an expert at that."

We parked in the alley and cut through our shop, then walked two doors down to Gold's.

When we opened the front door, a hubbub hit our ears, with at least twenty or twenty-five Warner Pier merchants already inside.

Garnet Garrett, our neighbor and Alex Gold's niece, was greeting guests at the front door, and she met each of us with a friendly hug. She thanked me effusively for sending the tray of chocolates. I assured her they were Aunt Nettie's idea.

"I am so excited about this summer," she said. "Last year was crazy, with our daughter's wedding, so this summer I'm looking forward to just staying in Warner Pier and working in the store."

"We're looking forward to having y'all around," I said.

"It will be great doing routine work. Back to the family trade."

"I didn't realize you had worked with jewelry, Garnet."

"Oh yes. All the Golds learn about jewelry at their mother's knee. I worked in Uncle Alex's Chicago shop for three years before I became a housewife. And I've worked in a couple of other shops over the years."

She leaned toward me. "Head for the second counter. That's where the mimosas are waiting for you two."

"Love those mimosas," Joe said. We walked toward the designated counter. Then he murmured, "Nothing like starting off a day of working with power equipment with a few glasses of champagne."

I chuckled as he asked the server for a glass of plain orange juice. I asked for the same thing. Then I whispered in Joe's ear, "I have the same concern you do. If mixing champagne with power equipment is dangerous, imagine what could happen to our finances if we mixed the bubbly with a computer. But this is high-class. They've even got champagne glasses for the teetotalers."

"Hererra's sent them," he said. "They've got all the catering tricks down pat. You can't tell who has champagne and who has juice."

We toasted each other with our plain OJ, then walked toward the counter that held food and other refreshments—coffee, sweet rolls, fruit, sausage, and bacon.

The shop looked beautiful. There were gorgeous flower arrangements and lovely silver pieces—everything you'd expect for the opening for an exclusive jewelry store. Alex was living up to his reputation as a prominent expert on antique jewelry.

And more people were coming in all the time.

Alex wormed his way toward us through the crowd, his small stature occasionally making him disappear in the sea of people.

I couldn't help kidding him. "Alex! This is scrumptious! But I thought you were going to open a shop that specialized in homey jewelry suitable for the beach!"

Alex was too excited to acknowledge the teasing. The small man strutted back and forth, seeming to stretch his height by several inches.

"Beach!" he said. "Beach is right! Every occasion—even a picnic—calls for the right jewelry! And we'll have it all. Make sure you stick around until nine o'clock. That's when I'll make the big announcement!"

Joe and I filled our plates and greeted our friends and acquaintances. The entire coffee club was there. Digger Brown was obviously holding a real mimosa, and I didn't think it was his first. "Hey, Joe," he said, "where are the doughnuts? I have R. L.'s doughnuts every morning."

"Gee," I said, "I'm glad my plumbing doesn't need attention today."

Digger grinned. "Your plumbing will be in good hands, I promise, no matter how many mimosas I have." He leaned close. "After noon I can call Superior Plumbing if I need a substitute!"

I looked up and saw Tony Herrera walk through the door. Joe waved to him, and I smiled as I saw that he and Lindy were actually coming in together. So often Warner Pier parties forced the two of them to attend separately because Lindy was in charge of the serving and the food. Today she had handed that off to their daughter Alicia.

I felt happy, surrounded by people I knew and liked. Had this Texas gal managed to become a happy camper in Michigan?

At one point when the group shifted, I saw what seemed to be the centerpiece of the entire party. At the back of the shop, higher than eye level, a glass shelf had been erected. On it was an even higher glass shelf, narrower and standing above the first one. The effect was of a dais—two shelves atop each other creating a dramatic stage.

For nothing. Neither shelf had anything on it except a velvet scarf.

What was that all about?

I immediately knew that Alex had some purpose for this odd structure. He had not simply forgotten to finish his decorations. And I realized then that most of the people there—the crowd had reached about thirty-five by then—were also noticing the empty centerpiece.

What was Alex going to put there? I was definitely planning to stick around to find out. Nine o'clock. That's when Alex had said he planned to make a big announcement.

I saw Aunt Nettie across the room. She was happily talking to a friend, but I saw no sign of Hogan. Hmm. I'd expected to see the two of them together. Then I saw the chief's patrol car go by. Apparently Hogan's responsibilities had made him late. I resolved not to let the delay titillate my curiosity and ruin my enjoyment of the breakfast.

Because it was really nice. In Warner Pier our social events tend to be casual. Hot dogs and paper plates. Rarely did we get cut glass, fresh flowers, elegant food, and mimosas. Even if Joe and I weren't drinking them.

I moved toward the front door to try for some conversation with Garnet. Joe followed me.

"What's going on?" I asked her.

She immediately looked suspicious. "What do you mean?"

"With Alex's big enunciation—I mean, announcement! What's he going to announce?"

"Another special event. And it is a big deal." Garnet glanced at her wristwatch. "I wish he'd go ahead and do it."

As if he had heard her, I saw Alex's head appear above the crowd.

"Good," Garnet said. "He's starting."

Alex was apparently on some sort of ladder, because his head and shoulders got higher and higher. He climbed toward the top, hooked a knee around one of the ladder's legs, and waved his arms. For a moment I feared that the whole apparatus was going to topple over, but it stayed erect.

"Okay!" Alex's voice was jubilant. "Now for the big event!"

The crowd applauded, and Alex leaned down. Someone handed him a large framed photograph, at least twelve-by-fourteen. Alex lifted it above his head, then turned from side to side, displaying it before the accumulated merchants of Warner Pier.

He called out in a loud, clear voice, "The historic jewels of the grand duchess!" Then he carefully placed the photograph on one side of the lower shelf.

Someone handed him another photo, and he repeated the procedure. This time he declared, "The historic jewels of the last czar." He placed the photo on the other side of the lower shelf.

A third photo was handed to him. This he declared "the historic jewels of the czarina!" And he placed the photograph on the top shelf.

And he didn't fall off.

I joined in applauding the feat. My applause was sincere. I'd been sure that Alex would land in a heap on top of one of the glass showcases. But, no, Alex was still standing on his ladder, and he was going to make a speech. Everybody fell silent.

"You're probably wondering why we're paying tribute to three photographs," Alex said. "But we're not paying tribute to the photos. We're paying tribute to the jewels displayed in them!

"In a week—only *one week*—the reproductions of the genuine jewels in the photographs will be displayed here in Warner Pier. These historical replicas of the famed jewels—on their way from Minneapolis to a two-month exhibition in Chicago—will make a three-day stopover right here in Warner Pier, in Gold's Jewelry."

Everyone applauded. I joined in. I did not care about fancy historic jewelry, but I liked Alex a lot.

And, of course, the purpose of Alex's participation in the tour was to promote his shop, not to sell the czar's jewels.

Hardly any of the tourists or summer people who visited Warner Pier would want to buy expensive jewelry, certainly not world-famous historic jewels. Their interests lay in moderately priced earrings and necklaces made by local artists. But an exhibition of priceless jewels would show the world we could appeal to the wealthy and connected as well as to middle-American families.

The crowd was breaking apart now, with some attendees congratulating Alex, then heading for the front door, likely going to their own shops. Garnet was still at her post, letting guests in and out, doing her hostess act.

I noticed Garnet shaking Hogan's hand as he left. Was Aunt Nettie with him? No, I saw her toward the back of the shop. Hogan was leaving alone. That seemed odd. I moved toward the front of the shop myself.

That's when I saw the car from the Warner County Sheriff's Department in front of the store. I rushed toward the door and followed Hogan out. He was approaching Sheriff Ben Vinton, who was just getting out of his car.

"Well, Hogan," Vinton said, "has your burglar finally been caught?"

I gasped. What was the sheriff talking about? Nobody had been arrested.

Almost immediately, however, I realized that the sheriff was not claiming that a burglar had been arrested. He was *asking*—asking if someone had been arrested. It was one of Vinton's usual stupid remarks. Of course, as soon as his words were repeated to the breakfast buffet in the jewelry store, the people inside rushed out and the people outside rushed in.

The report just about ended the festivities at Gold's Jewelry. Everybody wanted to know who had been arrested and how they got caught.

I felt sympathy for Alex; his big announcement was completely upstaged.

Then Hogan began a quiet conversation with Vinton.

Tony Herrera and Joe joined me, staring at Hogan and Vinton.

Tony murmured, "What's all this about, Joe?"

Joe shrugged. "I have no idea." He stepped aside and pulled out his telephone, punching in a number as Tony moved away.

I wasn't surprised to see Hogan glance at his own phone, or then watch Joe key in additional letters. I looked over Joe's shoulder and saw letters appear on Joe's screen, apparently replying to Joe's message.

"No," it said. "Talk to you later."

Joe nodded and turned away. Then he led me back into the jewelry store.

We were once again greeted by Garnet. "Sorry," Joe said. "Can I hide in your back room while I make a call?"

Garnet smiled. "Sure. Lee will keep us entertained."

I apologized to Garnet and Alex for dodging out of their grand-opening party early.

Garnet shrugged the whole thing off, but Alex wanted to talk about it. "Bill Vanderwerp tried to tell me the raccoon trapper, Watt Wicker, is the burglar." Alex sounded incredulous.

"That's what some people were saying," I said. "But I don't get it."

"He definitely wasn't one of the men who tied me up!" Alex sounded annoyed, as if he'd been assaulted by an impostor.

"They may try to say he was."

"But he's just not, Lee. He's the wrong size and shape. Too tall. Too skinny."

"I don't think Hogan thinks Watt has done anything."

Joe appeared from the back room, took my arm, and said,

"Come on, Lee, I told Aunt Nettie you'd be in soon, and we need to do an errand first."

Joe thanked Garnet and Alex for the use of their back room, and I gave them an awkward good-bye as Joe pushed me toward the street door. I could tell he had something on his mind, and it wasn't escorting me to my office.

"What's up?" I whispered as I followed him out. But he was silent as he rushed me through the TenHuis Chocolade building and loaded me into the van.

"Where are we going?" I asked.

"I called Watt," Joe said. "I'm still his lawyer. And he's not under arrest. He answered his cell phone from the hospital."

"So he's okay?"

"Right. Watt's mind is not extremely clear at the moment, but he told me one thing."

"What?"

"Wildflower," Joe said. "Watt said something like 'Go to Wildflower. She's got the trash.' I think we'd better get out there and talk to her ASAP. The cops didn't find anything at Watt's place, nothing to do with trash or anything else. But I'm thinking maybe he hid something at Wildflower's."

Chapter 21

We got into my van, and Joe left Warner Pier headed east. In about twenty minutes he pulled into the drive at Watt's place.

I was surprised. "Aren't we going to Wildflower's?"

"I thought we better make a quick check at Watt's first."

"We can't get into the cabin," I said. "I gave Watt's keys back to Hogan."

"We can get in. Watt told me where he hides a second set."

Naturally, Watt's place still looked like a wreck, just as the searchers had left it. We got out of the van and walked around a few minutes, just looking things over. Then Joe found Watt's hidden keys and unlocked the cabin's front door, and we went in.

The sleeping bag was still torn off the bed, the mattress was askew, and magazines were dumped on the couch.

"No trash in here," Joe said, looking around.

"Well," I said, "just like Watt told us, we're going to have to ask Wildflower."

"She seems to know everything else that goes on in this neighborhood."

"And she's got cell phone service." I pulled out my phone and called her. She answered on the third ring.

I put the phone on speaker and explained our problem. "We just want to make sure that when they searched Watt's place, the technical crew looked everywhere. And we wondered about the trash. But we can find hardly any! Did someone carry it off?"

Wildflower chuckled. "It's at my house," she said.

"Your house? Why?"

"Because around here, we're supposed to either drive it to the dump ourselves and pay them to take it, or we put it out for one of the commercial companies and pay *them*. Watt only had one bag a week—if that. So we made a deal. He did some gardening and digging chores for me, and I put his trash out for pickup with mine. It saves us both effort and money."

"And I suppose the official truck has already picked it up."

"Oh no. They don't come until tomorrow. You'll have to dig through it, but anything from his house ought to be over here."

"Be right there."

"Good. Because there's one kinda odd thing you might want to look at."

"What is it?"

"I'll show you."

We headed out of the cabin, and as we were locking the door, a Warner County Sheriff's Department car pulled in and stopped, blocking the drive. To my surprise, Sheriff Vinton got out.

Joe spoke to me in a low voice. "Keep your mouth shut."

More loudly, he spoke to Vinton.

"Hi, Sheriff. Do you patrol here?"

"Paige did, mainly. What are you two doing here?"

"Oh, the more we thought about the big search out here, the more I thought I'd like to look the place over peacefully."

Vinton smiled. "You mean you're double-checking the state police?"

"Not exactly. Just hoping that inspiration will strike. Do you visit the site every day?"

"Hey! The big commotion out here was only yesterday. I haven't been back since then. I asked all the deputies to keep an eye on the area, just routinely."

"Have you seen anything?"

"Only Mr. and Mrs. Joe Woodyard." He laughed.

Joe and I laughed, too. All three of us sounded uncomfortable.

"Everybody knows they're up to no good," I said. "It's sure been an odd situation lately."

Vinton nodded. "That poor ol' Watt can't seem to stay out of trouble."

"Yes," Joe said. "He's my client. I hope they'll keep him in the hospital, or wherever Hogan has him in protective custody, until they make sure he doesn't have any health problems."

Then he gestured toward the drive. "You going to let us out?"

Vinton agreed to move his car, and we followed him out to the county road. As we drove away, I started to call Wildflower to tell her we might be held up a few minutes. But Vinton turned his patrol car in the opposite direction from Wildflower's house and put his toe down. He went flying toward the sheriff's office while we drove sedately toward Warner Pier.

"Is Vinton going to circle around and try to figure out if we go anyplace else?" I asked.

"We've been friends with Wildflower for several years. I don't see how a visit to her would raise any eyebrows," Joe said. "We're right in her neighborhood. It's just a normal drop-in, right?"

Wildflower seemed happy enough to see us, and five minutes after our arrival, we were sitting on a tarp in her backyard with two black trash bags put to one side, and one white bag in front of us.

"This is what I wanted you to see," Wildflower said. She leaned down and turned the white bag over. It was taped shut, and on the side was a note, also taped in place. "Important! Keep safe." The only signature was a large *W* written on the tape beside the note.

Joe looked puzzled, and I'm sure I did, too. "Hmm," he said. He turned the sack over and over.

"I'm not about to open it," Wildflower said.

"I suppose that, as his lawyer, I could open it," Joe said. "But it might be smarter to put it in a secure place."

He stood up, carried the sack to our van, and put it in the front seat.

I could have popped him, just from pure curiosity and frustration. Wildflower looked as if she could, too. I was dying to tear into the white sack, and I'm sure she was, too.

But neither Wildflower nor I gave in to the impulse to do that, and after a few more minutes of looking in the trash bags, Joe and I thanked Wildflower and said good-bye.

Joe spoke as we drove away. "The boat shop! That's the place!"

"The place for what?"

"Opening that sack! Aren't you dying to see what's in it?"

"Of course I am, Joe! But you said . . ."

"The boat shop is the nearest place I can think of where we can be undisturbed. I was dying to open it at Wildflower's. But we couldn't take the risk of that idiot sheriff interrupting us."

Laughing, I slid the white trash bag under my seat and tried to act calm while Joe took the van past the Rest-Stop and to Joe's shop. He pulled into the drive, and we ran into the shop's interior workroom.

"Lock the door," Joe said. "Just in case."

"What's in this?" I said. "It sure is heavy."

We took it to a worktable and cleared space, then dumped a heavy book out of the sack. It was about an inch thick, about twelve inches tall, about nine inches wide, and had thick covers.

"It's a photo album!" Joe said. "And it's got a nice little place to put a photo on the cover."

But there was no photo there.

There were four or five dozen photos of people—men and women—wearing military garb. Some had names underneath—names or nicknames. G.I. Joe, the Beard, Bad Boy or Sgt. Roy Spence. Holcolm.

The album had been treated with care—until it was tossed in with Watt's trash.

I almost whispered. "What a nice album."

"It sure seems like something that was prized and kept carefully."

"These are nice photos, too," I said, turning the pages. "They were taken by a professional-quality photographer using a good camera. This is a record of someone's army service."

There were pictures of men—and some women—receiving medals or standing beside military vehicles and other equipment with their arms around each other's shoulders. Eating at formal luncheons or in extremely informal mess tents. Some of the subjects were smiling, some were glaring.

"I can't look at the whole thing right now," I said. "But we can take it away. I mean, you have Watt's authorization to do that, right?"

"Oh, sure," Joe said. "I'm still his attorney." Joe and I looked a bit more, then repacked the album into the white garbage bag. We left, mystified, taking the album with us.

"I wonder," I said as we drove toward the chocolate shop. "I wonder if Watt took these photos?"

"Why do you ask?"

"Because he does take photos. On his phone. I've seen him do it."

Joe didn't answer. As he turned down Peach Street, he pointed at a jazzy red pickup parked in front of TenHuis Chocolade.

I gave a yelp. "Hey! There's Mike's truck! He and Dolly must be back. I hope they got an okay from Hogan!"

I picked up the album, still in its bag, and we went in our back door. I'd expected that Mike and Dolly had gone up to her apartment, but they were standing in Aunt Nettie's alcove office off the kitchen, talking to her. We all fell on one another's necks with sincere greetings.

"We got Hogan's okay to simply keep a low profile," Dolly said. "We'll just be careful!"

Aunt Nettie frowned at Joe and me. "Where have you two been?"

"We went back out to Watt's cabin to see what else was there," Joe answered.

Mike looked at him sharply. "Find anything?"

"Nothing that explains anything. Just something that's even more mysterious," Joe said.

I held out the heavy album, still in its bag, and Joe laid it on the corner of Aunt Nettie's desk. He peeled the sack back, revealing the album, explained where it had been, and read off the message on the bag's front.

Aunt Nettie said, "My goodness!"

I said, "We couldn't believe it."

Joe said, "It was a big surprise."

Dolly said, "Who would even pretend to throw out something like that?"

Only Mike didn't say a word.

His face was furious. Everyone was silent for a long moment.

Then he spoke. "I told you there was no reason to drag all that up. It has nothing to do with this. I'm sure. Positive."

Worth the Suffering?

(The Chocolate Moose Motive)

Our grown son was home for the holidays, and in an after-dinner discussion, he mentioned that chocolate caused him to get sores on his tongue. Then he reached for a piece of Gran's Fudge, a particularly creamy and luscious candy our family makes at Christmas.

"Hey!" Mom cried.

Son shrugged. "It's already sore," he said.

Well, he's an adult. If he's willing to suffer so he can eat fudge once a year, that's his choice.

But many people have problems with chocolate. It can cause heartburn or migraines or worsen arthritis. Some people are out-and-out allergic to it, just as they may be to any substance.

I'm sorry about that.

For everyone else, here's the recipe.

Gran's Fudge

4½ cups sugar

1 large can (10–12 ounces) evaporated milk

1 jar (7 ounces) marshmallow cream

18 ounces semisweet chocolate chips

2 tablespoons margarine
1 teaspoon vanilla
Dash salt
2 cups chopped pecans

Mix sugar and milk. Cook over medium heat, stirring frequently, until the mixture reaches soft-ball stage, about 10 minutes or longer. Remove from heat. Add marshmallow cream, chocolate chips, margarine, vanilla, salt, and pecans. Mix until smooth. Pour into a 9-inch-by-13-inch buttered dish. Let set 24 hours.

Note: Everyone in my family uses an old-fashioned pressure cooker pan to make this. No, we don't use pressure. We just use the pan because it's heavy and suitable for extra-hot ingredients that shouldn't be burned or scorched. I'm lucky enough to have fallen heir to the actual pressure cooker my grandmother used, and I prize it.

Chapter 22

Mike's snarl had been directed at all of us, but his gaze had been aimed at Joe.

We all stared in response. Aunt Nettie's face screwed up as if she might cry. Dolly looked shocked and hurt. I'm sure my mouth was gaping open with surprise.

Joe was the only person who didn't change his expression. "Drag what up?" he asked. "Why did Watt try to hide the album?"

Mike's reply was a deep sigh. Then he sat down in an office chair beside Aunt Nettie's desk, leaned back, and crossed his arms.

"God knows why Watt does anything," he said. "I know Watt is kind of an oddball. But people shouldn't always be trying to push him around."

Joe remained absolutely calm. "How long have you known Watt?"

Mike threw his head back and spoke defiantly. "Since he came to Warner Pier," he said.

"Then how do you know that people 'always' push him around?"

Mike's gaze fell, and he took a deep breath. "Okay! Watt and I were in the army together. That was fifteen years ago! And, yeah, he was odd then, too. Several of us got in the habit of kinda taking care of him."

He looked up, glaring at Joe. "But Watt never did anything, you know, *wrong*! One time some guys tried to get him involved in a robbery, but he just called me and told me about it. I took him to the MPs. Watt's problem is that he never seemed to catch on to things."

Joe nodded. "Did he serve his full enlistment?"

Mike shook his head. "He was released, 'for the good of the service.' It's not a dishonorable discharge. He just didn't fit in."

Joe didn't reply, and in a moment, Mike gave a deep sigh. "I liked Watt," he said. "He was always out in left field, of course, but sometimes he saw things a lot clearer than the rest of us. And he's not stupid! Just in a different world."

"Why didn't you want to tell people you knew Watt? Dolly says you didn't tell her."

"It was Watt who didn't want me to tell anybody. I guess he was embarrassed because he'd always been the oddball in every situation. So he stuck to himself. A real loner."

Joe frowned. "Then why did Watt hang on to this album?"

"That? That's mine! And it really is a prized possession of mine." Mike took a deep breath. "I—well, I treasured the album. Watt made it for me after he and Bob pulled me out of that chopper—barely got me out before I was barbecued! I owe him a lot!"

Mike was staring at the book. "Watt borrowed it last week.

I don't know why he wanted to see it, but I sure didn't expect him to hide it in the trash."

Joe nodded. "Do you mind if I look at it?"

For a moment I thought Mike was going to refuse. But he didn't. "I don't mind," he said. "But I don't see any reason that you should."

"It might shed some light on Watt. On his character and background."

Mike shrugged casually, but he pursed his lips firmly. "Sure, you and Hogan can look it over. As long as I get it back! And I promise to talk to Hogan about Watt. Once I get a more important chore taken care of."

Our little welcome-home session for Dolly and Mike ended with that. Mike still looked mad, and Dolly still looked puzzled.

Everyone but Aunt Nettie and I left. Dolly promised to be in for work the next morning. Mike promised to see Hogan. And Joe left without saying where he was going. He put the photo album back in the garbage bag and left with it, telling me he was taking my van, but he'd be back to pick me up at five.

We had never gotten around to lunch, and it had been a long time since the goodies at Gold's Jewelry open house. So I drank a Diet Coke, munched a handful of cheese crackers, and ate a double-fudge bonbon ("layers of milk and dark chocolate fudge with a dark chocolate coating") to tide me over until my next meal, whenever it arrived.

I would also have liked a nap, but I gave that idea up, just the way I gave up worrying about that photo album.

I did manage to accomplish several things—I did the paperwork for a big order of Halloween candy for a Chicago department store—they expect their ghosts and goblins to arrive long before Labor Day—and discussed our information storage situation with Bunny. The afternoon dragged on. Finally it actually crawled past five o'clock, and I was still there waiting for Joe to pick me up. He had my van, and I was wondering if I'd have to ask Aunt Nettie to give me a ride home. She was packing up her belongings, getting ready to leave.

At last, the phone rang, and the caller ID said, "Joe." I clutched the receiver to my ear. "I'm hungry!" I said.

"Yes, it's been a long time since our champagne breakfast, hasn't it? I've spent the whole afternoon looking for Hogan, and I still haven't seen him."

"Could we simply go home?"

"Actually I just found out where Hogan is. How about asking Aunt Nettie and Hogan out to the house for dinner? I'll pick up some fried chicken from Herrera's, plus a salad."

"I can make a salad. But what makes you think you can find Hogan now?"

"I'm holding on his line while I talk to you on mine. Oops! There it goes."

My phone went silent and began to blink, telling me I was now the one on hold. And in a few minutes Joe was back. "Hogan says yes to dinner," he said.

"I'll invite Aunt Nettie."

My placid and agreeable aunt said yes, and shortly afterward, she and I were in her Buick sedan headed for our house. We got there about ten minutes before Joe and Hogan arrived. Aunt Nettie and I indulged in a glass of wine, and the guys came in with a six-pack of Labatt's. All of us were tired, but the prospect of a friendly talk seemed to spread happy feelings around the dining room.

As soon as we'd each taken a piece of chicken, I spoke. "Can we talk business while we eat?"

Everybody agreed.

"Then I claim the first question," I said. "Going back a couple of days, how the heck did Watt get away from Mike's cottage so he could wander the streets?"

We all looked intently at Hogan while he chewed and swallowed. "I have no idea," he said. "It's a complete mystery."

"Hogan!" Joe, Aunt Nettie, and I all howled his name. Then Aunt Nettie spoke. "You still don't know?"

"No, I don't. Watt swears that the last thing he remembers is being at the cottage. It was about nine or ten a.m. He was drinking a cup of tea. Mike had just left to buy cereal."

Hogan looked at Joe, frowning. "Watt's apparently sort of famous around Herrera's for preferring hot tea to coffee. Anyway, he woke up on Van's roof with no idea how he got there. And his watch read four p.m. He climbed down one of the ladders from the roof and began to try to get someplace—either back to Mike's or to his own house."

Joe frowned. "What do you *think* happened?"

"If Watt really has no recollection of how he got there or how the day disappeared, then someone must have drugged him. It would be pretty easy to put him on top of the building, where Darcy and Katy thought they saw him. I have an idea, but I can't prove it."

"And your idea is . . . ?"

Hogan shrugged. "I think somebody managed to put a sleeping pill or some similar substance in his tea, probably after Mike left the cottage. Then, after Watt fell asleep, that somebody, or possibly two somebodies, carried him up there."

Aunt Nettie broke in. "But, Hogan, Watt hadn't been in Warner Pier long. Who did he know who would help him get—well, anyplace? Especially up on the roof."

"That's a good question, Nettie."

We discussed it for a few minutes. If Watt needed help leaving the hiding place Hogan and Mike had arranged for him, or if someone had kidnapped him, who could it have been? Or put another way, who might have contacted him and offered to take him someplace?

Could it have been someone who worked at one of Mike Herrera's restaurants? Lindy or T. J.? Someone else? No one seemed likely. Watt presumably had acquaintances, but none of us knew who they were, and Watt wouldn't talk to Hogan about it.

The conversation faltered. Joe and I had had such a crazy day that we began to falter, too. The food was gone, so Hogan and Aunt Nettie left. I tossed the paper plates into the trash and wiped down the kitchen counters.

As I made a final circuit of the downstairs before turning in, I noticed that Joe had held on to the photo album. It was still wrapped in its white garbage bag and was on the corner of the coffee table.

Sighing, I sat down, unwrapped it, and took it out. I idly began to turn the pages of the book.

Mike's album was a very ordinary photo album. Any captions were informal, mostly the nicknames I'd noticed earlier. No one was identified formally. Instead, each photo was marked with information like f-stops and exposure times.

Certainly, Watt had unexpected talents.

I closed the album and headed for bed. I'd think about it tomorrow.

I went into the bedroom, gave Joe a kiss on the forehead—his only response was a gentle snore—then climbed into bed. My plan was to snuggle down under my quilt and drift off to sleep. It was a cool night with a pleasant breeze, and the windows were open.

But Joe had gone to sleep and left my bedside lamp on, and the light didn't seem to be bothering him. My notepad was on the side table. I decided that I could make some notes and write out some questions I'd like answered. There were more than a few.

Chapter 23

First question: What were the Cookie Monsters after? These prowlers had gone all over our small-business community, breaking into a dozen stores and taking nothing but crackers and cookies. Why on earth would they do something so pointless? They could shoplift similar snacks from any grocery store with a lot less trouble. So what were the burglars after? Were they planning a more serious crime? If so, what was it? What was here in Warner Pier that someone would want to steal?"

Second question: If someone had drugged and kidnapped Watt and put him someplace he didn't want to be, who had it been? And how had they managed it? Or was Watt wrong about being kidnapped?

Third question: What did these people have against Watt? Why was he getting this treatment?

Fourth question: What did these people have against Mike? Mike was also something of a stranger to Warner Pier. How had he managed to draw someone's anger? Was it his job as night patrolman that did it?

Fifth question: Besides Watt, Alex Gold was the only other person who had been molested in any way by the Cookie Monsters, when they locked him in a closet. Why? We had all assumed that he surprised them inside his store, and they reacted by imprisoning him to keep him from raising an alarm. But why would they do that? If the Cookie Monsters were just pranksters—kids prowling around, maybe—why didn't they simply flee when he surprised them? Kids could easily outrun a man in his sixties. And attacking an older man who was not a strong physical specimen was a serious crime.

Sixth question: Were the burglars skillful? Or were the burglars simply bumbling around? Then I answered my own question—yes, they were skillful. They could pick locks, for example.

Seventh question: If the burglars did have skills, what were their limits and capabilities?

Eighth question: What skills did each of the burglaries require? Could that information help to narrow down suspects?

Ninth question: Who was Bob?

I laughed at the last question, of course. Bob was merely someone who had hired Mike to do an odd job and was slow to pay.

Mike was apparently the only person who knew who Bob was, and he must have promised to keep his argument with Bob quiet. Then, with his usual lack of impulse control, he had talked loudly in the Rest-Stop about the situation. Their argument could be about anything, or nothing, but it involved money. No one but Mike and Bob knew what Mike had been hired to do.

Maybe the mysterious Bob wanted a special liquor cabinet

in his boat. Or maybe he wanted a piggy bank shaped like his boat or a playhouse for a grandchild. Maybe the project was to be a surprise for his wife.

Why did Bob's identity obsess me? Mike had just laughed the question off. But something about the way he ducked his head when Bob's name came up . . . I wanted to know!

I had written each question on a separate sheet of notepaper, and now I rearranged them, putting them in what I would call order of importance. Actually in an order that piqued my curiosity.

The most important question was the first that occurred to me: What could anyone want to steal in a resort town whose shops specialize in casual clothing and relaxing goods such as books, lawn chairs, and secondhand furniture?

Not a dang thing! Maybe antiques? Artwork? But small stores didn't carry valuable items like that.

And interestingly, no private homes had been hit by the Cookie Monsters.

But there had been a big announcement earlier that day. Next week, we would have some famous, valuable jewels on display in Warner Pier!

At the moment, Warner Pier shops had nothing to draw professional thieves. But for three days next week, we'd have reproductions of some of the world's most exotic jewels.

And the historical replicas would contain actual jewels—not fake ones. Brides-to-be could have diamond rings that were copies of the last Russian royal jewels, set with real diamonds, rubies, emeralds, and sapphires. And, yes, we had families in Warner Pier who could afford to buy these gorgeous gems. We had grooms who could offer their brides three or four acres of land on the lakeshore. Such a gift could conceivably be valued at half a million or more. They could certainly offer their brides an impressive diamond or three.

Gold's Jewelry would stock or order them. The jewels would be burglar bait. The czarina's jewels might draw thieves the way a tree full of nuts would draw squirrels.

I got so excited that I got out of bed and walked all around the bedroom, kitchen, and living room. And as I walked, I muttered, "I have to talk to Hogan! I have to talk to Hogan!"

Finally I got back into bed, trying to lie still and not disturb Joe.

"Hogan must know!" I told myself. "Hogan must know!"

At this point Joe turned over, scooted toward me, and spoke.

"You're so sexy when you mutter," he said. "Then I know that you've made some great discovery." He kissed my neck, right under my ear.

I tried to tell him about it, but he kept kissing me, and I lost all track of my reasoning.

I had it back by the time we were at the breakfast table, however. Over coffee, I showed Joe my notes and outlined the things I would like to talk to Hogan about.

"Not that Hogan hasn't already thought about these things," I said. "He's a professional, after all."

Joe nodded. "Yes, he probably has. But it wouldn't hurt for him to know that somebody else has figured it out as well."

He chuckled at the "Who's Bob?" question and nodded at the query about the czarina's jewels.

"But the item that intrigues *me*," he said, "is the question of what skills do the Cookie Monsters need? I've been fascinated by the way they seem to enter through locked doors."

Joe picked up his cell phone and dialed a number. "How about we ask Hogan to drop by and talk to us?"

And Hogan agreed to come.

This surprised me. Why should an experienced detective like Hogan agree to listen to the ideas of two amateurs? Of course, Joe had some experience as a defense attorney, but he's not a detective. And when it comes to solving crimes—well, I may have figured out a few problems in our small town, but I don't pretend to be an expert.

But Hogan came to our house, drank our coffee, and patiently listened to my ideas and to the ideas Joe had added to mine.

When we'd covered all our notes, Hogan nodded. "What you're telling me," he said, "is that you think the Cookie Monsters may have been practicing on the businesses around Warner Pier, waiting for an occasion such as the exhibition of jewels at Gold's new store. And that the exhibition may enable the Monsters to become serious thieves and make a try at stealing the valuable collection."

"We could use the jewels as a trap!" I said.

Then the three of us began to laugh. We couldn't help it—we finally felt as if the Cookie Monsters could be caught!

So, with laughter and doughnuts, we figured out a story. "I'll tell everybody that I've decided these break-ins and the attack on Watt are obviously simply jokes," said Hogan. "Maybe talk to some of the town's known pranksters and let people think they were questioned about it."

Joe and I would spread the word in case anyone in Warner Pier didn't already know about the jewels, and we would vigorously deny that we had gotten any information from Hogan. And if the press asked questions, as they might, Hogan would deny any idea that a major robbery was likely to occur.

Joe grinned. "The Cookie Monsters haven't attempted such a high-profile crime before, so we'll say we don't expect this to be any different."

Anyway, that was the plan. Hogan would tell Alex Gold but no one else. It was, he said, worth a try. We were all still laughing as Hogan and Joe left for their respective offices.

"The jewels are supposed to be here Tuesday, Wednesday, and Thursday," Hogan said. "So if you have to hint at dates, those are the ones."

I was scheduled to work from two p.m. until ten that night, so after our meeting with Hogan I had time for a little housework. I loaded the dishwasher, made the bed, and went back into the living room. There I noticed Mike Westerly's album, which was still sitting on the coffee table. On impulse, I picked it up, and I decided to waste ten more minutes looking at it. Maybe it could reveal something more.

After going through every one of the pages, I noticed one face popping up repeatedly. And I realized that I had a new suspect.

Chapter 24

If there's anything I hate, it's running into people that I *recognize* when I can't remember *how* I know them. I don't know their names, I don't know where I met them, I don't know who the heck they are. But they're familiar.

I don't know if I went to high school with them, if I occasionally see them in the produce aisle at the grocery store, or if they're nurses in my doctor's office and know more about my body than my husband does. They're familiar, yet not familiar enough.

Once I ran into the television weatherman twice in one afternoon. I greeted him effusively each time, then realized that, while I had seen him frequently, he had never seen me.

It was humiliating.

That's what happened with that darn photo album. Most of the people in it were, of course, complete strangers to me, people Mike had known in the army years earlier. But there was this one guy—one guy—who was incredibly familiar.

All I could tell was that he had light-colored hair and light-colored eyes. He seemed to be unusually tall, but in most of the pictures he was sitting down, so I might have that wrong. His head was sort of square. He had a crooked grin that might knock some women flat and a way of giving the camera a sideways glance that was provocative and attractive. Who was he? I knew him, but how?

The first photo in the book had Watt in it. Then came two guys who didn't trip any recognition wires, and then Mr. Familiar.

If there was a common denominator in the pictures, of course, it was soldiers in uniforms. And the square-headed guy with light eyes. Next in number came army equipment. Then houses that were definitely not in the United States. Then deserts. Next, helicopters. And, after that, Mr. Familiar again. He was in at least a quarter of the pictures.

Who did I know who had been in the army? Was he someone I had known in Texas? Someone from Michigan? From college? From an office where I had worked? A restaurant where I'd waited tables? From Holland? From my teenage days when Lindy and I hung out at the Warner Pier Beach?

There was one other hint. Mr. Familiar must have worked with machinery. Actually with more than machinery. He seemed to work with any sort of tools or gadgets or electronics. In every photo, he was screwing things, sawing things, nutting and bolting things, assembling things.

But where had I seen him? Where had we met? What had we been doing that made him so identifiable, yet so *un*identifiable?

Of course, I told myself, if this album belonged to Mike, then that should give me a clue—Mike must know him, too. But when I tried to picture the few of Mike's friends whom I knew, this guy did not pop up as a member of the group. The only pictures my subconscious dredged up included people like Dolly, Joe and me, Lindy and Tony, and other ordinary people around Warner Pier. Mr. Familiar did not appear. All that proved was that he didn't live in Warner Pier. Yet—yet—yet—well, it seemed as if he ought to.

I tried to eliminate some categories. He didn't ring the bell as a member of the Warner Pier Rest-Stop coffee club. I couldn't associate him with any of the downtown stores. He didn't pump gas at a Warner Pier gas station or make change at the community theater. Nor did he take my order for lunch or carry groceries out to my car or cut my hair.

I finally spoke aloud. "I guess I'll just have to ask Mike who the heck he is."

Then I gasped. Next, I murmured, "Oh my gosh! Mike said this was his album. But there's not one picture of him in it!"

Not one picture of Mike. Well, maybe that was because Mike took all the pictures. Then he couldn't be in them.

But that didn't sound right either. This album was pictures of friends. Friends hang out together, saying, "Hey, guy, take one of all of us with my camera."

And this album had lots of such pictures. Groups eating in the mess tent, climbing on tanks and helicopters, working on trucks, playing cards, posing with their arms around one another's shoulders, snoozing on cots.

Like Mr. Unidentifiable, Watt was in about a quarter of the shots. But there was not one picture of Mike.

Yet Mike had claimed the album was his.

Did it matter? Possibly not.

Should I tell Hogan about it? Yes, I decided.

I picked up my phone and called Dolly at her desk. It was only fair to warn Mike. And there was no point in hesitating.

Dolly answered on the first ring. "Hi," I said. "Is Mike there?"

Dolly's voice was hesitant. "He's supposed to come over. He should be here any minute."

I tried to make my voice firm. "Well, tell him not to leave. I'm on my way, and I need to talk to him, too."

I hung up. It would be much better for Mike if he admitted to Hogan that he'd fibbed about the album himself.

If the album had any meaning at all, then Hogan needed to know about it. And if it didn't—well, then why had Watt tried to hide it?

When I got to TenHuis Chocolade, Mike's flashy red pickup was sitting in front of our shop. *Good*, I thought. I drove into the alley and parked in my own spot, picking up the white plastic sack that still held the album.

Dolly was standing on her tiny balcony. As I got out of my van, her eyes dropped to the sack.

She leaned over the railing and spoke. "Mike was right. He said you would be the one who looked the pictures over carefully enough to notice anything."

I went up the stairs and into her living room. Mike was standing in the middle of the floor, waiting for me. I held the album up to display it, but I didn't say anything.

Mike shrugged.

I spoke. "This album sure confused me." I dropped the book onto Dolly's coffee table and dropped myself onto the couch. "I've never run into anyone who owned a whole album without one photo of himself in it. And there was one other thing."

As soon as I had the book out of the sack, I flipped it open and tapped my finger on a photo on the first inside page.

"Mike! Who the heck is that guy?"

Mike stared at me, then he laughed harshly. "You don't recognize him? I've done all this worrying, and you don't even recognize him?"

"Mike!" I held up one fist and shook it, then winked like Popeye. "Unless you satisfy my raging curiosity, nobody's going to recognize you! Who is it?"

"You're going to feel dumb when I tell you." He grinned and sat down beside me. "Add a beard."

"I imagined that. It didn't help."

"Add thirty pounds."

Heavier and with a beard. Who could it be? "He was in the army with you?"

"He was a sergeant. He and Watt and I got acquainted with each other because we had all spent a lot of time in Michigan."

"But you didn't tell the world about it. Why would you try to hide a friendship?"

"Some guys you just owe. When our chopper went down, he and Watt pulled me out of it. Through flames. I'd be dead if they hadn't done it. I owe them."

"But what are you trying to hide? Who is it? You're driving me crazy!"

Mike looked through a few more pictures, grinning. "I've given you some hints. Think about it! Meanwhile, I'll take the album over and explain to Hogan. I'll tell him why I fibbed about owning it. And I still find it hard to believe there's anything wrong."

I closed the album and put it back in its plastic sack. "Here,

Mike. But I'd really like to understand why you went to all this trouble for this guy and what you hoped to accomplish."

Mike frowned. "Basically, I don't want to be the reason somebody looks up his record. Or Watt's. I'm pretty sure Watt is in the clear. And I thought the other guy was, too. But if not, he can take care of himself."

"But what's to know?" I asked.

"His record! Lee, the guy has a record! He's been to prison! He got a dishonorable discharge! I don't know if he did anything wrong or not. But knowing he has a record is going to put him at the top of the suspect list for whatever the hell is going on in Warner Pier!"

Mike left, leaving Dolly and me alone. She sank into a chair.

"Honestly! Will Mike ever learn to act like a normal person?"

"Don't ask me, Dolly. I like Mike a lot. But some people always have a lot of excitement going on in their lives. Mike may be one of them."

Dolly jumped to her feet. "Oh, Lee! That buyer from March's Mercantile called this morning. We gotta talk about that!"

That was a signal for a discussion of a chocolate buyer who was an expert in her field, but who—like Mike—lived a truly dramatic life. I'd learned to listen to Dolly calmly, but the buyer still could send Dolly into a tizzy with a choice between milk chocolate witches with brooms or dark chocolate cats with pumpkins.

I thanked my lucky star that the two of them didn't have to discuss things very often, and I let Dolly tell me the entire tale. This required about ten minutes of concentrated listening before I ended the talk with a promise to call the woman back and try to calm her down.

Dolly had just reached a reasonable level of emotion when we heard more excitement.

"Hey! Hey!" We heard a loud yell from outside. Then the sounds of a scuffle.

Dolly jumped to her feet. "That sounded like Mike!"

She ran toward the back of her apartment with me at her heels. She shoved the door to the little balcony open, and the two of us ran onto the porch.

Below us, in the alley, was a white panel truck. A man wearing a light-colored canvas hat was slamming the double doors on the side.

Inside I could see feet, big ones, made even larger by a pair of enormous work boots. They weren't moving. I recognized those boots. They belonged to Mike.

Both Dolly and I screamed. "Mike! Mike! Let him out!"

The man in the canvas hat jumped into the driver's seat of the truck, and the vehicle dug out.

Chapter 25

I nearly did a swan dive off the balcony. But I had enough common sense left to realize that would probably break my neck. So I ran back to the living room, grabbed my purse, dug for the car keys, dropped them, fell to my knees and scrabbled around until I got hold of them, leaped to my feet—nearly knocking Dolly down the stairs—ran down the steps, and sprinted out the back door.

I'd been clicking my electronic car door opener as I ran, so I swung the van's door open, leaped into the car, and backed out of my parking place—once again almost killing Dolly, who was jumping into the other side of the van.

We tore out of the alley, but by then the white van had completely disappeared. I was muttering its license plate number to myself as I drove. One advantage accountants have in a car chase is that numbers are easy for us. We can remember the license numbers of the cars we're following.

We called 9-1-1 and reported the kidnapping while we drove around Warner Pier, looking for a white van. On every street corner we yelled at someone standing there, "Hey! Have you seen a white van?" Then I'd holler out the license number. Of course, nearly everyone had seen a white van, since they are incredibly common. Hardly anybody could remember the numbers.

After a couple of blocks, of course, a patrol car from the Warner Pier PD caught up with us. But that meant we had to stop and explain the whole thing, and it slowed the chase up. It was terribly frustrating.

We kept after it. The Warner Pier Police, the county cops, and the state police helped. We turned the streets of Warner Pier into a pinball machine, with my van and at least a half-dozen cop cars bouncing around, back and forth, trying to find that van.

We started the chase about eleven a.m., and by noon we still hadn't found them.

By then Dolly and I were tired out and at the ends of our ropes. And Mike was still missing. The white truck must have slipped into a hiding place.

"The van's simply got to be downtown," Dolly told me. "There's no way it could get onto the interstate or some country road before we were ready to take off after it."

"Hogan's checking all the downtown garages and other possible hiding places," I told her. "That van's got to be somewhere. And it didn't have very long to get out of the area."

"Yes, I know it's got to be here," Dolly answered. "It's so frustrating to feel like we're right next to it, but can't find it."

By twelve fifteen Dolly and I were sitting in the break room at TenHuis Chocolade, thoroughly discouraged. We stared at the walls, we looked at a city map, we even checked the aerial views from Google Earth, and we couldn't figure out how that van managed to disappear.

"In a flash!" Dolly said. "All my life I've heard of things happening 'in a flash!' But this is the first time it's actually happened! Right before my eyes!"

Every cop in southwest Michigan was looking for that van and for Mike, whom they considered a fellow officer.

The only good thing was that the kidnappers had not taken the photo album. We had found it under the steps leading to the TenHuis back door. Dolly and I guessed that Mike had managed to toss it under there as he struggled.

Joe kept calling for updates. He had headed for his office in Holland that morning, running late after our talk with Hogan. Naturally, after the kidnapping, I had Dolly call to tell him about it while I drove up and down the streets of Warner Pier, looking for the van. But Joe couldn't just drop everything—such as representing a client before a judge—and rush back to Warner Pier to help search.

But he did give me an idea. An unlikely one, but an idea all the same.

When we were talking about how the white van disappeared so quickly, Joe chuckled and said, "Maybe they got away by water."

"Or maybe they've hidden the van at your shop," I said. "It has plenty of space, and all the locals know where it is."

"They'd have to get inside."

"That would be no problem at all. The property owner—a guy who looks a lot like you—hides his key in a magnetic box he puts behind a downspout. Any burglar could easily find it."

"Yes, but it's awfully convenient when he needs to ask his wife to look for something there, and she left her own key at home."

We didn't laugh, because we were too worried about Mike. But sort of joking about Joe not locking up securely planted an idea in my brain.

The idea kept eating at me. But I kept working on finding Mike. *That's stupid*, I told myself. *After all, Joe is the nephew-in-law of the chief of police. And the son-in-law of the mayor. Nobody would use his shop as a hiding place.*

Or maybe it would be a smart place to hide a kidnap victim. If the crooks didn't plan to leave him there long. The shop had no close neighbors; nobody could hear a kidnap victim yell.

But it was nearly a mile from our alley to the shop, and that mile was full of turns and obstructions. Slow driving. They wouldn't have had time to do much before the cops were on their tail.

But Vintage Boats—Joe's shop—would have had plenty of space. If Joe could work on a thirty-foot boat in it, some bad guy could definitely hide that van there.

But by now, I told myself, the kidnappers had dragged Mike out of the van and had crammed him in some other vehicle—a pickup truck, a compact car, a giant Caddy, or maybe a semi. Finding the white van probably wouldn't help at all.

Once again, I consulted the Google Earth map that showed the streets, roofs, and alleys of Warner Pier. If you wanted to go from TenHuis Chocolade to Vintage Boats by the shortest route, how would you do it? I was surprised by the answer. It wasn't as far as I had thought. It was well under a mile. Not a fun drive, true, but not far.

The suggested route ran three blocks north and a half block right, then whipped onto the main road into Holland. It crossed

River Drive, then turned onto the far end of Dock Street. From there it would be two blocks to the riverbank, ending with a turn into the boat shop itself. And the whole route had plenty of trees and bushes for a van to hide behind.

But it would be useless, I told myself. There was no way that the white van or any other vehicle would be there. With Mike inside or not.

I got up from my desk and walked around the shop for a few moments. I ate a truffle, but after I swallowed it, I couldn't remember what flavor it had been.

Finally I decided that I had to know if it was possible for the van to get there so quickly. I got my purse out of my desk drawer and called out "Tell Dolly I'll be back in a few minutes" to Aunt Nettie. Then I headed out the back door.

I started my van and backed it out. I wrote the time down, took a deep breath, and started.

I only hoped that I didn't kill anybody with my little experiment. It was going to mean driving fast on a crowded route.

Gunning my van out of the alley, I barely slowed at the street, then flew straight across it and entered the alley in the next block. I kept going, traveling as fast as I could until I reached the next street. Again, I barely paused, took a quick look—left, then right—and made sure that street was clear. Then I sped into that alley.

At the next street, I threw on the brakes and waited for traffic to clear. There were only three cars coming, and since I was turning right, I didn't have to check the northbound lane. I swung a sharp right and headed north. Four more blocks—with only one brief pause—and I was chugging across River Street.

A quarter of a mile straight down Dock Street, then a final turn into the boat shop's drive, and I skidded to a stop beside Joe's big metal building.

I had hurried through nearly every intersection without paying real attention to traffic. My heart was pounding.

I checked my watch. I had made the trip in four minutes and forty-five seconds.

Now for one final push. I turned off the car, yanked the keys out of the ignition, and jumped out of the van. Luckily, I had the key ring with my keys to the shop in my purse. I pulled them out, ran for the side door, unlocked it, turned the handle, and yanked the door open.

And I could hear the sound of a car's motor.

How could that be? The building should be empty.

But behind a door in the back wall, the one that hid the storage area, a motor was running.

Something was wrong.

I pulled my cell phone out and called 9-1-1. The rest of the trip I'd be connected to the dispatcher.

I tried to tell the dispatcher I'd found the man every officer had been looking for, but I'm afraid my words weren't coherent. I muttered as I ran across the shop and threw open the door to the storage room.

A bright red pickup, a great big sucker, was parked inside. It was rocking back and forth gently, and I could smell exhaust fumes.

There's No Chocolate in Potato Soup!

(The Chocolate Bunny Brouhaha)

In several of the Chocoholic books, the characters eat potato soup. No, I haven't found a chocolate version.

But potato soup is close to the ultimate comfort food for my real-life family. And I've never eaten any as good as my mom's. The recipe is totally flexible.

Family Favorite Potato Soup

Potatoes, 2 medium-sized for each serving
Onions
Carrots
Celery (optional)
Chicken broth
Butter
Salt and pepper
Milk—evaporated, regular, or skim—cook's choice
Garnishes
  Sharp cheese, grated
  Green onions, chopped
  Ham or dried beef, chopped

The "2 medium potatoes" is a guide, not a rule. Add other vegetables in the amounts that look good to the cook. Peel and chop the vegetables into pieces of similar size. Put raw chunks in heavy kettle and add chicken broth, not quite covering. Bring to a boil and simmer, uncovered, until vegetables are quite soft. Do not drain.

Remove kettle from heat and mash vegetables with potato masher. I prefer the vegetables slightly lumpy. Add lump of butter, then salt and pepper to taste. Stir in milk, making the soup a bit thin, because it thickens as it sits. If this happens, add more milk or broth. Reheat over low temperature; do not allow to boil.

Each person can add garnishes to taste. Serve with soda crackers or whatever appeals.

Chapter 26

My first thought was that the van had turned bright red.

I'd traced the route of the white van, but I'd discovered Mike's flashy, bright red, enormous pickup—gaudy bed cover, gigantic tires, fancy steps, and everything else.

I didn't stop to figure how it got to the boat shop. At the moment all I could think about was getting the pickup's engine turned off.

I couldn't see inside the vehicle at all, front seat or rear. The sides and the back door were made of solid metal. The windows to the driver's cab had dark tinting. The whole population of Warner Pier could have walked by the truck and not noticed that there was a man inside it. I frantically banged on the side of the pickup and called out for Mike.

For a panicked moment I could not remember where the garage door opener for the room was located.

Then I realized that I was standing right beside it. I punched it, and the door went up. Blessed daylight flooded the workroom.

A long rubber hose was coming out of the exhaust pipe. I took six steps and yanked it free.

The hose was snaking along the side of the pickup and into the driver's side window. The window was almost closed, pinching the hose, but the hose kept the window partly open. My heart lurched.

I tried to open the driver's side door, but it was locked. So I didn't wait around to try the other doors of the pickup. I ran into the shop and found a heavy hammer on the main workbench. I used it to whack a hole in the window on the passenger's side of the pickup. Three blows and the whole seat was covered with shattered glass. I reached inside the window—thank heaven I'm a tall woman, because the vehicle sat up high—and unlocked it. Then I ran back to the driver's side, opened the door, and turned the ignition off.

Finally I looked into the back, terrified that I'd see Mike's dead body.

Instead I saw him in the back of the pickup, peering at me from between the seats.

"Mike!" I yelled.

He was wrapped in a quilt of some sort, his face just visible. Duct tape was wrapped around the whole affair, and Mike's body was held rigid with straps that reminded me of the bound feet of a Chinese princess.

Mike looked like a big puffy ghost. The blanket—or whatever it was—had a blue background and was stitched back and forth like a quilt.

The part nearest me seemed to be covering a head. A hole gave me a look at a face, and a pair of boots—scuffed, dirty boots—stuck out the other end.

And the boots kicked.

"Mike! It's you!"

I heard the sound of words.

"Thank God it's you, Lee!"

"I'll get you out!"

I rushed into the main shop and stared at Joe's tools until I found some tin snips hanging on a pegboard.

"I'm coming!" I hollered as I snatched them down.

I ran back to the truck and began cutting the duct tape off, starting at the top of Mike's head. I had to be cautious to avoid trimming Mike's beard, but within seconds his face was fully visible.

"Thank God, Lee!" Mike said. "They got the jump on me. I didn't know Bob had a pal!"

"Who? Who did this?"

"Bob! The shoe shop guy! His cousin. Bob! R. L. Lake! He was the guy in the album."

R. L. Lake. The cousin of Bill Vanderwerp. It had never occurred to me to wonder what the *R* and the *L* in his name stood for. Now Mike gasped two words out. "Robert. Lee. In the army we called him Bob."

Mike's hands were free by then, and he rubbed the back of his head with them. "They gave me a bad headache! But it took two of 'em to wrap me up."

When I began to try to cut Mike free, I discovered that one of the strips of duct tape attached him to some hooks in the bottom of the truck bed.

The cops seemed to take forever to get there, but was I glad to see them. Warner Pier Police arrived first, closely followed by the town's volunteer EMTs. Hogan assumed command of the crime scene, naturally, and kept nearly everybody out. Word must have spread rapidly, and people who knew and cared about

Mike pulled in, with Dolly and Joe in the lead. They parked out on Dock Street and lined up, wanting to see him. Dolly was one of the few Hogan allowed in.

Why hadn't Mike died of carbon monoxide poisoning? That's what I kept asking—first myself, then the EMTs and cops. Why was he still alive?

Carelessness, Hogan told me. The gap in the window let air into the pickup.

"Maybe they were just in a hurry," he said. "Or maybe they were overconfident. If they'd looked around in the shop, they'd have found that big box of rags Joe has. They could have stuffed them in the crack in that window. Closed up the crack. Then Mike wouldn't have made it.

"But as it was, the fumes had to fill that giant garage before . . ." Hogan quit talking.

When he started again, he asked a question. "But who did this?"

"Bob. R. L. Lake," Mike said. "The doughnut guy."

Hogan frowned. "R. L.? 'The doughnut guy'? Do I know him?"

Jerry Cherry answered. "Sure, Hogan. R. L. Lake delivers doughnuts around Warner Pier for Hole-n-One Donuts." He leaned closer and lowered his voice. "R. L. is Bill Vanderwerp's cousin."

Hogan's voice dropped to a whisper. "Lee, can you shut up about this?"

I nodded, and Hogan headed out. I knew he was off to check records. It was a letdown of sorts when Jerry told me that though I'd have to make a statement, nobody at the police department had time to take it right then.

"You and Joe go home," he said. "Just don't make any deductions, okay? And definitely do not talk to anybody!"

We obeyed. We collected Aunt Nettie at the shop and took her home with us. When dinnertime came, I made potato soup. If my grandmother's recipe wouldn't soothe me, I don't know what could.

To further the evening, the state police took over the hunt for Bill and R. L., so Hogan was also able to get away and join us.

And when the phone rang, it was Alex Gold. Joe answered, and Alex said he was calling to make sure I was all right.

"She's right here," Joe said. "Cooking dinner. Are Garnet and Dick there? No? Come over and eat with us."

It didn't take much to get him to agree. And it was truly comforting to be eating with friends and relatives after the excitement of that day.

As we sat down at the table, I took a deep breath and sprinkled sharp cheddar into the soup. "I guess we shouldn't talk about all this, but I know we're all thinking about it. I just hope they catch those guys before they do any more harm."

Aunt Nettie sniffed. "I'm going to smack that Mike Westerly's bottom! He should have told us all he knew about Bob or R. L. or whatever they called him. And all about whatever the trouble was he had in the army."

"Aw, Aunt Nettie," Joe said. "He was just trying to be loyal to an old army buddy."

"Well, he sure learned something."

I laid down my soup spoon and stared into my bowl. "I hope he did, because I sure didn't. I don't understand anything that's gone on. Oh, I understand that Bill and R. L. seem to be the bad guys, but I'm completely in the dark about what they did, why they did it, and how they wound up in this mess. Not to mention how the rest of us wound up in it with them!"

Aunt Nettie smiled at Hogan. "Maybe Hogan can explain it. After he eats his dinner."

"You'll have to eat fast, Hogan!" I gave him what I hoped was an imploring look. "What's going on, anyway?"

"I agree that it's very confusing, Lee." Hogan smiled. "I admit I have some inside information that helps me."

He sprinkled sharp cheese in his soup. "Maybe it will be better if we try it chronologically."

"Beginning when?"

"How about two teenage cousins who kept getting in trouble around twenty years ago? Their mothers were sisters, but from what I hear, the sisters were very different. One spoiled her son, and the other didn't. In fact, she was extremely tough. But both boys turned out selfish and both got in trouble."

I narrowed my eyes. "I assume you're talking about the Vanderwerp cousins."

Hogan nodded. "We don't need to go into all their early escapades, but one of them wound up in the reformatory and the other—the one most people thought was luckiest—was allowed to join the army. Both actions were attempts to straighten them out, but neither worked. Which is a sort of tragedy, since both Bill and Bob were intelligent and both had outwardly pleasing personalities."

"But, Hogan," I said, "they *killed* people."

"Yes, but maybe they wouldn't have . . ." He shrugged and went on. "Anyway, they stayed friendly with each other, even though they didn't continue to live in the same area. Bill, of course, kept in touch with his parents—who were likely to leave their property to him. R. L. was forced to leave the army because of his crimes, and his civilian career also includes a prison term for theft."

He paused, emphasizing his next words. "But the army is where Bob met Mike and Watt. And, yes, the three of them really did get involved with each other because two of them were from Michigan and the third had spent his childhood summers here in Warner Pier.

"The link was cemented by the crash of the helicopter. Army records show that Mike—the pilot—got a medal for bringing the chopper back to base and landing it under fire. Bob and Watt—members of the ground crew—climbed aboard and pulled injured members of the crew off the chopper. These included Mike. Mike was seriously wounded and eventually left the army because of resulting disabilities.

"He was still hospitalized when Bob—R. L.—was accused of theft again. Watt, with his innocent view of life, didn't really catch on to what R. L. was up to when his fellow Michigander talked him into helping. But Watt was uneasy enough that he confided the whole plan to Mike. Mike immediately caught on and saw that Watt went to the authorities. R. L. was court-martialed and bounced from the army. Watt took a discharge 'for the good of the service.' Mike now says that R. L. promised to reform and showed evidence that he was doing so. But his subsequent activities don't indicate that he really intended to do that."

I stared into my soup bowl. "Especially with Paige," I said. "I feel sorry for her. I guess she was dating Bob, and he . . ."

Hogan lifted his eyebrows. "We're just guessing about what

happened with Paige, Lee. But don't feel too sorry for her. I'm afraid she was a full partner in the scheme."

I shook my head. "But, Hogan, what was the scheme? You've told us all about Bill and Bob, but we don't know what they were up to."

Hogan laughed. "Alex, you know more about it."

Alex smiled, but his expression was more rueful than amused. "I guess I goofed," he said. "I'd been told that if a merchant had some unusually valuable item in stock—such as replicas of some historic jewels—it was smart to alert law officers about keeping them safe. I had some routine business with Vinton anyway, so like a good little boy, I asked him who I should talk to about the valuable jewelry I was going to show." Alex shook his head. "I sure learned a lesson!"

I gasped. "Was Vinton involved?"

"Not directly," Alex said. "But Vinton didn't know what he should do, so he picked up the phone and called somebody."

Joe rolled his eyes. "Oh, gee, Alex!"

"Right! Oh, gee, Alex, indeed. Everybody in the sheriff's office could hear him talking about the Russian jewels!"

"Including Paige," Hogan said. "I'm not sure just how it happened, but apparently this was exactly the type of opportunity that Bill and Bob had been keeping an eye out for. Paige probably told them about it the same day."

He frowned. "What came next is the part you can pity Paige for. As nearly as I can tell, Paige thought that a jewel robbery would be a lot of fun. Like a caper movie. But she wasn't ready to kill anybody."

"Oh!" I gasped so loud that everybody stopped talking and looked at me. "I just remembered something."

"Well, what was it?" Joe asked.

"The night we all stayed at the hospital to see how badly hurt Watt was, about five in the morning Paige came in and joined me. Mike and Joe had gone to get coffee. Just after she came, they returned, and when she saw them, she almost screamed. Gave a big—a sort of a gasp." I dropped my eyes. "I never saw her again. Bill and Bob must have killed her that morning."

Hogan nodded. "She wasn't reliable. They used the complicated plan, the same one they later used on Mike, to kill her, faking her death as a suicide."

"They were the 'lumpy' figures?"

"The lumpy business was those moving pads they used to tie her up. They used duct tape over those to wrap her without leaving marks. Today they used the same method on Mike."

"But where did the photo album fit in?" Joe asked.

"That I can answer," Hogan said. "Watt told us the whole story this morning. The album originated as a gift for Mike, something his former outfit wanted to send him as a souvenir. Watt took nearly all the photos. But they couldn't get any photos of Mike, because he'd been evacuated to a stateside hospital."

"I'd learned that Watt was a talented photographer," I said. "And I guess that R. L. knew it, too. But here in Michigan, years later—well, who cared?"

"R. L. did," Hogan said. "You see, after moving back to Michigan, Mike ended up in Warner Pier. He had kept in touch with Watt, but both had lost touch with R. L. and that guy had no idea Watt and Mike were both here. When R. L. moved to Warner Pier, he realized the three of them were sure to run into each other, so he contacted Mike and told him a good lie. He assured Mike—his former commanding officer—that he had reformed. His life of crime was over, he said. Mike didn't want to be buddies with him, but he also didn't want to discourage him from straightening out if his intentions were legit."

"That's like Mike," Joe said. "I've always found him to be a genuinely nice guy."

"Right," Hogan said. "On the other hand, Mike was cautious about R. L. From what you guys say, the two of them occasionally came to the coffee club, for example, but it was unusual for them to show up the same day."

"Yah," Joe said. "I've noticed that if one of them came in late, the other one was likely to leave almost immediately. But why did that matter with the album?"

"R. L. made a casual call on Mike and discovered that he had the souvenir album prominently displayed at his house. R. L. didn't want another casual visitor to look at it and discover that he and Mike had a history."

Joe frowned. "Why would that matter?"

"I don't think it would have, unless R. L. had another plan. One that boded no good for Mike."

We all sat silently, taking that in. Finally I saw all the implications. "Oh, golly!" I said. "R. L. must have planned to kill Mike!"

Hogan didn't speak, but the rest of us did. We buzzed like killer bees.

In a minute, Hogan went on. "I'll never be able to prove that. And it would never matter unless Mike and Watt were linked. But somehow R. L. was inspired to go out to Watt's cabin to find out if another copy of the album existed. And he discovered—it did. Watt had one. When R. L. left, he stole it.

Took it with him. And Watt knew he was the only person who could have taken it, and wondered why.

"Watt's an unusual guy, as we all know. Mike says he is 'smarter than he seems,' and that's a pretty good description. Watt never understood why R. L. was interested in the album, but was afraid he was up to no good. So he borrowed Mike's album, and then he hid it at Wildflower's house."

"Well, I feel like an idiot," I said, "because I didn't recognize Bill when Dolly and I actually saw him drive off with Mike in the back of the shoe store van. And I feel even dumber for not thinking about Mike's truck disappearing."

"Where was the truck?" Alex asked.

"It was parked in front of TenHuis Chocolade," I said. "I saw it there."

Hogan nodded. "But as Mike left you and Dolly, he stopped to talk to Bill and R. L. I guess he was going to warn them they'd better forget their plot. Anyway, they attacked him, dragging him into the white van. One of them then went around to the front of TenHuis—taking Mike's car keys—and drove off in his truck. Then Bob took Mike's truck out to Joe's boat shop."

"Gosh!" I said. "Dolly and I wasted all that time looking for a white van when we should have been looking for a red truck!"

Joe shook his head. "They wouldn't have switched Mike from the van to the truck until the truck was hidden at the shop," he said.

Alex took a piece of stuffed celery from the relish plate. "I just couldn't picture Bill and Bob as burglars. They look and act so innocent!" He bit the celery with a decisive snap.

I guess we were all a little giddy. I know I felt great relief knowing that the Vanderwerp cousins were behind all of this, and soon, they would be detained. I felt as if the entire adventure was over. Solved. Just an unhappy memory.

Until Hogan's cell phone rang. "Excuse me," he said. "I'd better get this." Then he pulled the phone out of his shirt pocket.

"Jones," he said. We all sat silently while he listened, frowning. "What's that?" More listening, more frowning.

I was beginning to feel nervous. "I'll get everybody away," he said. Then he clicked the phone off. "Okay," he said. "Everybody get ready for a new emergency."

"Oh, surely not!" Aunt Nettie said. "Can't we have a calm dinner?"

"Not yet, Nettie. That was the state police. By the time they got warrants for R. L. and Bill, both of them had disappeared."

A chorus of "Oh no!" broke out. Hogan held up his hands for silence. "We need to get all you witnesses to a safe place."

Chapter 27

That got our attention.

A chorus of "What's happened?" went up.

Hogan sighed. "The state cops were keeping an eye on the shoe store, and they were positive that the two of them were in there. But when they went in, the building was empty."

Joe stood up, frowning. "Do the state cops think you're all in danger? Because the Vanderwerp boys are probably mad as hops."

"It seems silly, Joe, but he seems to think Alex is, and quite possibly Lee." He turned to Aunt Nettie. "And he doesn't like the idea of them taking an interest in my wife either. Just on general principles."

When Hogan's words sank in, I nearly went into a fit of fear on Aunt Nettie's behalf. I could feel shivers begin to run up and down my backbone. Surely no one could want to hurt Aunt Nettie.

Or Joe. Or even me.

"What does he want us to do?" Joe said.

"He's sending a patrol car, and the officer will escort you to a safe place."

"It may be overreacting," Joe said. "But I guess we'd better cooperate."

The calm and reassuring way that Joe spoke made me feel certain that he thought there actually was danger. I didn't like that.

Joe and I collected a few of our belongings—money, prescriptions, jackets. Since it was already evening, it was possible that we'd be gone overnight, but we didn't take pajamas. Joe and I assured Aunt Nettie and Alex that we'd stop for their essential belongings on the way to the police station. Since Alex lived just down our drive and across the road, he had to be convinced that he could not simply walk down there and pick up his toothbrush. But he didn't argue very hard.

Joe was completely calm until I poured the leftover soup into a saucepan and stacked the dinner debris in the sink. Then he almost yelled at me. "Lee! We can't take time to do the dishes!"

I began to laugh, maybe just a little nervously. "Don't be silly, Joe. I'm just putting up the soup so we can reheat it later. If I have time before Hogan's patrolman gets here, I might put the dishes in the sink to soak."

He put his arms around me and whispered. "I don't mean to snap. You already gave me one scare today, gal, when I found out you went off after Mike. I can't take two." I gave him a big hug in return.

Alex called his niece and her husband to tell them he was leaving their house, and to urge them to stay away, too. The girls in charge of the chocolate shop called Aunt Nettie to say they were closing our shop early at the request of the police, and that they'd been offered escorts home.

"They're clearing the whole block!" Dale said. I couldn't tell if she was scared or thrilled.

We were all ready by the time two patrol cars pulled into our drive. A state policeman with MABRY on his name tag loaded Aunt Nettie and me into his car, while Joe and Alex climbed into a WPPD car driven by Patrolman Jerry Cherry. The two patrol cars stood by at Alex's place—actually his niece's house—while Alex hurried in to pick up his necessary belongings. And our little cavalcade went on. All of us stayed calm.

That's when Aunt Nettie asked if she could stop by Ten-Huis Chocolade, instead of her house, where Hogan had directed our escorts to take us next.

A radio discussion ensued, but Aunt Nettie quickly shut it down. "You tell Hogan," she said firmly, "that the final two employees left the shop only fifteen minutes ago. I find it hard to believe that two crooks could have broken into our shop to ambush us since they left. My blood pressure medication is in my desk drawer, and I promise to be into the shop and out of it in two minutes. Lee can come with me."

Hogan gave her his approval, telling the state cop that our block had been cleared and that he believed it was safe. Then I grabbed my purse, since I'd need my keys to get in. Aunt Nettie and I got out of the patrol car, and the two of us went in the front door of the shop and back to the workroom, where she has her own special alcove. Our state police escort accompanied us but stopped to wait by the front door.

Aunt Nettie found the prescription in her center desk

drawer with no problem. She was just tucking it into her purse when, at the back of the building, the door that leads to the upstairs opened.

I wasn't frightened, but I was surprised. The only thing that door leads to is Dolly's apartment and, another story higher, the roof.

I called out. "Dolly?"

I had assumed that Dolly had accompanied Mike to the hospital in Holland. Now I wondered if she had stopped at home for some reason. Had the police missed her when trying to empty the block?

"Dolly? Are you here?" I turned around to see if she had come out of the door from the upstairs.

And I found myself staring at Bill Vanderwerp and his cousin R. L. Lake—also known as Bob. Now I realized that he must be the "Bob" Mike Westerly once threatened.

I nearly had a heart attack.

Bill and Bob were walking toward us, coming through the break room and into the workshop. Both were grinning, smiling ear to ear with their innocent Dutch faces.

If I had had a pistol, I would have shot both of them. What right did they have to enter *our* space—the workroom of TenHuis Chocolade—and frighten my aunt and me?

Looking back, I see that it was extremely lucky that I did not have a weapon. Because Bill and Bob had two.

Both were holding pistols—square-shaped, shiny, silver pistols. And those pistols were pointed at us. If I had had a pistol, I might well have pulled the trigger right then. But for an inexperienced shooter like me to hit anything—well, that's unlikely.

A gunfight, which might have grown to include the police outside, was more probable.

So all I did was step in front of Aunt Nettie, and the two of us faced Bob and Bill defiantly.

"Ladies," Bill said placidly. "What's the best way out of this place?"

"The front door," I said. "But you'd better put the pistols down first. There are police officers out there."

Bob gave a harsh laugh. "I don't like that idea. How about a basement exit?"

Aunt Nettie gave a sniff. "The only exit from the basement is the door you just came out of. The landing you crossed has access to both the upstairs and the downstairs. Plus, it crosses the door to the alley. And that door is where all the rear exits are."

"Then it looks like it's going to be a tough way out," Bill said. "I hope you can duck fast."

He raised the pistol, and for a moment I thought he was really going to shoot us.

But Aunt Nettie spoke quickly. "Wait! Lee, I asked you to check the roof. Is there any way out up there?"

"You can *get* to the roof," I said. "Getting off it might be a bit harder."

Bill flashed a look at Bob. "Well, we made it from our place to here by way of that roof," he said. "Plus, there's that ladder down at the end."

"Maybe we can get to the other end of the block, break into the apartment down there," Bob said.

Bill nodded.

The most chilling part was that they were so calm. They acted as if they were planning a picnic, not escaping from the police who were after them for the murder of Paige.

But they had stopped the quick glances at each other and were looking at us. Calmly and directly, they stared at Aunt Nettie and me.

"Well," Bill said. "You ladies get your jackets."

"You don't need to take us along," I said.

"I'm afraid we do," Bill said. "There are cops in the area. We need someone to go along with us."

"As shields?" I tried to make my voice sound unbelieving. "We'd only slow you down."

"Shut up!" Bob barked out the words, and Aunt Nettie jumped.

Bill grumbled impatiently. "I told you, we've got to get going. Get your jacket."

"Mine is in the locker room, at the back," I said. I'd nearly told them the truth—I didn't have a jacket. But then I realized that a jacket might be a good thing to have along. I couldn't scoop a pistol, a machete, or a rock out of nowhere to give myself a weapon. But if things got desperate, I might be able to hit Bill or Bob with a jacket to distract or blind one of them, or—by golly!—scratch one of them with a zipper.

"That's right on our way," Bill said. "Come, come, ladies."

"My cane's here," Aunt Nettie said.

I stared at her, but I managed to keep my mouth shut. Her cane? Aunt Nettie never used a cane.

But as she came from behind her desk and began to walk toward the corner of the room, I saw that she was limping. She picked up a cane—a slender one with a hooked handle—from the corner hat tree. It was the one I'd found on the roof, the umbrella she had wrapped with rubber bands so that the shredded cover wouldn't flap.

I wondered why she wanted to bring along a broken umbrella. Maybe to use as a potential weapon? I didn't know how that would stand up against two loaded pistols, but I kept my mouth shut.

Besides, I had to worry about my own lie. The light jacket that I had picked up at home was in the patrol car on the street in front of the shop. All I could do was hope that somebody, anybody, had left a jacket in the closet off the break room.

And then the second miracle of the day happened: There was a jacket hanging in the locker room closet. It was a blue denim jeans jacket that belonged to Bunny. The jacket came nowhere near fitting me, but I hung it over my arm, trying to look confident.

We started for the door where Bill and Bob had come in. They motioned for us to go first, and the four of us started up the stairs.

Of course, I was familiar with that landing, the one in front of Dolly's door. A second set of stairs went down the front way, to the street. Behind us was the solidly built door that led to the stairway up to the roof. I produced the keys from my purse and started to unlock that. Then I realized that door was already unlocked. Bill and Bob had apparently come into the shop through it.

I hesitated there, and Aunt Nettie followed my lead. But a few nudges from Bill's and Bob's pistols started us climbing, feeling our way up the dark stairs.

Now was the time that any weapons, such as jackets or

keys or canes, would come in handy. If one or both of the Vanderwerps weren't looking at us, we could hit them with the cane, gouge an eye with a key, or simply throw a jacket over someone's head and shove them. Preferably down a steep set of steps.

But again, no such opportunity arose. Bill grabbed Aunt Nettie's upper arm and held her firmly with his left hand while he stuck his pistol in her back with his right hand.

He looked at me. "Act right, or your aunt gets it," he said. I acted right.

Once we came to the door at the top of the stairs, Bob used his cell phone as a flashlight, and I opened the door that let us onto the roof. The door swung back, and we stepped outside.

There was plenty of light there, thanks to the streetlights that bordered our block, and Bob turned his cell phone flash off.

Bob crawled over toward the parapet around the edge of the roof. We heard a shout from the state policeman who had accompanied us into the shop. "Hey! Where'd they go?"

We were almost directly over his head, but neither of us said anything. Bob got to his feet, and he and Bill began to hustle us to the corner, the one nearly a block away. All of us knew there was a fire escape–type ladder down the side of the wall at that corner.

Bless Aunt Nettie's heart; she was a wonderful actress. She stumbled along, keeping the limp absolutely realistic. I tried to do my part to make it convincing by saying "She can't run!" in a thick whisper.

When we came to the next building, Bill even put his hands under her arms and gave her a jump, the kind you'd give a child, to move her across the little parapet and onto the next building.

They kept us moving briskly. Once Aunt Nettie stumbled, but one of them caught her before she fell down.

Finally, we were at the end of the block.

And the distraction that we needed had not yet occurred. Aunt Nettie and I had not been able to make a break for it.

Bill and Bob located the spot where the ladder went over the back of the building.

"I'll go," Bob said. "Tell me if it's clear. Then I'll pull the ladder down, and I'll get the ladies over the edge."

Bill knelt near the parapet. He listened. He turned his head back and forth, checking. Apparently he couldn't see anybody. He nodded to Bob, then turned himself around and sat on the edge of the parapet.

That's when the third miracle happened.

As he sat there, the branch of a tree hung over Bill's head, a branch of an ornamental tree growing beneath us in a hole on the sidewalk. Bill reached up and grabbed the branch. It bounced.

And as it did, a raccoon jumped out of that tree and scurried across the roof.

That darling animal scared the whatever out of all four of us.

Bob let go of Aunt Nettie's arm.

She swung that umbrella like a baseball bat and hit him in the ribs with all the power that a sixty-eight-year-old woman can muster. He fell over backward, and she hit him in the head with the crooked handle, stunning him.

Bob lost hold of his pistol. I kicked it across the roof.

Then I threw that jacket I'd been carrying through all this, dropping it over Bill's head.

He was so startled he let go of the parapet, slipped down the ladder, and fell two stories, feet first.

Aunt Nettie and I both began to yell at the top of our lungs.

Chapter 28

It was twenty-four hours before I could talk rationally about that episode of my life, and to this day, if I try to discuss it, most of what comes out is gibberish.

After Aunt Nettie and I managed to beat the Vanderwerp cousins into nerveless pulps, everything went mad.

The men downstairs—including both our husbands—couldn't figure out where we were. They could hear us screaming, but our trek across the roofs had led us a half block away, and they couldn't find us. And when they did find us, they couldn't believe what had happened.

Aunt Nettie, of course, was the heroine of the hour. That she had managed to convince Bill and Bob that she (1) needed a cane, and (2) had one that just happened to look a lot like a broken umbrella—well, it sounds like the dumbest thing in the world.

She had a simple explanation. "I guess it was dark," she said.

And I suppose she was right; the cousins simply couldn't see what she was carrying in any detail. She said she had a cane, and it looked vaguely like a cane, so they believed her.

I didn't get nearly as much praise and attention for merely dropping a jacket over Bill's head and kicking Bob's pistol thirty or forty feet. But my attack on Bill did leave him with two broken legs. I tried to feel sorry for him. But maybe I didn't try as hard as I could have.

And my wonderful aunt Nettie will always be a heroine to me.

As soon as Bill and Bob were off the scene, Watt slowly joined life in Warner Pier. He still lives alone in the cabin in the woods and does chores for Wildflower. He also caught the raccoons under our porch and took them to safety in the Fox Creek Nature Preserve.

Shortly after Mike Herrera came back from his trip, a job as a cook opened up in one of his restaurants. He hired Watt. So now Watt still works hard, but he is usually home by midnight. And he and T. J. are still pals, and T. J. talked a high school friend into taking the summer job cleaning kitchens.

Watt's also still taking pictures. In fact, he recently won a prize from a wildlife publication—for a darling photo he took of a mama raccoon with six babies.

As for why Watt was kidnapped, it was simply because Bill and Bob thought he knew too much. Or so we all think. Watt had, over the years, caused Bob a lot of trouble, and I believe Bob simply decided to get him out of the way.

The czarina's jewels, of course, were never in Warner Pier. As soon as Alex and Hogan realized the danger of theft was real, about a day after Paige's body was found, Gold's Jewelry had lost its stop on the tour. Alex got high marks from the police for continuing to pretend the famous jewels were still coming.

But Alex says the czarina's jewels will be back next year. "And the previous plot to steal them will be fabulous publicity!"

One other interesting event happened after all the ruckus died down. Mike was out of the hospital in a few days, and he and Dolly quietly got married.

They're now living in Mike's house and making plans for a big remodeling project on his cottage. They're happy, and we're happy for them.

But when I'm working on the TenHuis Chocolade budget, and I need a quick estimate about the amount of chocolate required to produce a hundred pounds of bonbons, I sure do wish I could just holler up the stairs to Dolly.

Acknowledgments

With many thanks to friends and relatives who have helped me with information for this book. They include lawman Jim Avance, Michigan neighbors Tracy Paquin and Susan McDermott, banker Joan Houghton, security company veteran Jerry Houghton, retired master sergeant Terry Anderson, truck expert Aaron "Shug" Shugard, photographer Jeff Dixon, and chocolate expert Elizabeth Garber.

In addition, the Lawton, Oklahoma, Arts for All organization once again sponsored an auction in which donors bought the right to have their names used in the book. Thanks to Barbara Boguski for a generous gift honoring Dale Nomura.

I also received help and support from my husband, Dave Sandstrom, and our three kids: Ruth Anna Henson, John Carl Sandstrom, and Betsy Jo Peters.